MW01252029

Mary had thought she made a good match, but now he was dead, and she didn't even qualify for a widow's pension…

No morgue was inviting. This one was no exception, just a bleak little building with barred windows, behind St. Anthony's hospital. The two women gave Harold's name to a severe-looking woman behind a glass partition and were told to wait. After what seemed an eternity, a small man in thick spectacles and a white coat came out to speak to them. "I'm sorry I can't give you the death certificate, it's already been picked up, and Mr. Porter's remains have been taken away," he said pompously.

Maggie was the first to take this in. "What do you mean, we can't have the death certificate? My daughter's his wife! And where have you taken him?" she blustered.

The man in the white coat turned red in the face and stuttered "I—I'm sorry, his wife—"

"His wife? I'm his wife," whispered Mary.

"I'm sorry" he began again. "The woman who came had the marriage certificate, dated 1902."

Four women journey through life between 1905 and 1945—a mentally, physically, and financially draining period, leaving behind the Boer and Crimean wars of the late 1800s, thrust too soon into WW1, the Crash of 1929, and then just ten years later, WW2. Women had to be strong, raising their voices to be heard, coping with loss, deprivation, and fear. Follow Colette, railing against the constrictions of an Edwardian lady's life; Mary, facing the future as a single mother; Emily, a wheeler-dealer gambler used to getting her own way; and Joannie, an innocent denied her biological family. Will she ever know the truth?

KUDOS for *The Train Now Leaving*

In *The Train Now Leaving* by Vivienne Barker, we follow the lives of four extraordinary women from 1905 to 1945, through the trials and tribulations of war, economic disasters, and family problems. Colette, in 1905, is struggling with the constraints put upon women by the strict Edwardian society in which she lives, after immigrating with her husband and two young boys to London from Belgium. From Colette's high society, we move to Mary's East End poverty-stricken life, facing the future as a single mother after the First World War. Then we follow Emily and Joannie through the tragic consequences of World War Two, culminating in a surprising tie in of all the plots together. Even though the story moves from one plot to another and through a fairly long period of time, it's quite easy to follow, and the various subplots and characters are fascinating. It almost seems to be a first-hand account of what it was like to live in that time. I thoroughly enjoyed it. ~ *Taylor Jones, The Review Team of Taylor Jones & Regan Murphy*

The Train Now Leaving by Vivienne Barker is the story of how two families' lives intertwine over the course of several years from 1905 to 1945, through wars, financial and emotional disasters, and the ends and outs of daily living, along with all the problems associated with your station in life. Whether rich or poor, Barker's characters all faced a myriad of problems—many tragic and poignant—that real people face. Barker writes with a unique voice that makes the reader feel as if they are right there with characters going through the harsh realities of a country at war. From petty discriminations to dishonest spouses, from suffering with PTSD to having your home and all your possessions blown to smithereens by an enemy bomb, these people were a much sturdier lot than most of today's generation—no matter what life threw at them, they just kept muddling through. A very thought-provoking and entertaining read. ~ *Regan Murphy, The Review Team of Taylor Jones & Regan Murphy*

ACKNOWLEDGMENTS

My thanks to the Bobcaygeon Literary Guild for their encouragement and guidance.

THE
TRAIN NOW
LEAVING

VIVIENNE BARKER

A Black Opal Books Publication

GENRE: HISTORICAL FICTION/HISTORICAL ROMANCE/WOMEN'S FICTION

This is a work of fiction. Names, places, characters and incidents are either the product of the author's imagination or are used fictitiously, and any resemblance to any actual persons, living or dead, businesses, organizations, events or locales is entirely coincidental. All trademarks, service marks, registered trademarks, and registered service marks are the property of their respective owners and are used herein for identification purposes only. The publisher does not have any control over or assume any responsibility for author or third-party websites or their contents.

THE TRAIN NOW LEAVING
Copyright © 2017 by Vivienne Barker
Cover Design by Jackson Cover Design
All cover art copyright © 2017
All Rights Reserved
Print ISBN: 978-1-626946-65-1

First Publication: MAY 2017

Published by Black Opal Books **http://www.blackopalbooks.com**

DEDICATION

To my grandchildren Emily and Gavin, that they may
know the people in their past.

CHAPTER 1

Arrival

London 1905:

Finally, it had stopped raining. After three days, the torrents had ceased, and a watery sun was half-heartedly trying to dry the glistening cobbles. As the hansom cab pulled up to their new home, two boys whooped with joy and tumbled out onto the pavement. Their parents descended somewhat more sedately, but both were relieved to have finally arrived. Bags were unloaded in front of a flight of stone steps leading up to the imposing black front door—the boys already at the top, were eager to enter. Their mother, still standing on the pavement, turned around to take in her new surroundings.

Colette was reluctant to live in London. It was always exciting for a visit and shopping, but was gray, damp, and seemed shrouded in fog most of the time. This was somewhere very different from her small home town of Spa and the lush forests of the Ardennes.

Franz had insisted on leaving. He assured her that life was only going to get worse for the Jews in Europe, and, even though he was non-orthodox, his business was suffering as customers began to shun them, if only to preserve their own skins. It was time to move for the boys' sakes.

Franz took a large key from his coat pocket and, opening the double doors wide, beckoned his wife up the steps. She climbed slowly, taking in the elegant row of Georgian houses, wrought iron railings, steps leading down from the pavement to the servants' domain, and the unexpected quiet in the middle of the biggest city in Europe.

"The furniture will arrive momentarily, my dear, but I have to go to a meeting, and I'm already running late. I hate to leave you, but I'll return as soon as I can. I'm sure the boys will help, and the moving men will just need direction. It will be fine," he reassured her.

Colette was too stunned to speak. This was just too much. She had no idea of the layout of the house, but Franz was already dashing out of the door to his meeting. As he was about to step into the still waiting hansom cab, a large covered wagon, drawn by two magnificent shire horses stopped behind him.

"Mr. Leyh?" inquired the driver, stumbling over the pronunciation of the name.

"Yes, yes, that is I, but I'm afraid I'll have to leave you. My wife is inside, ready to direct where the furniture is to go. Please speak to her." And, with that, he jumped into the cab and was off down the street.

The burly wagon driver lumbered up the steps, and, seeing a woman he presumed to be Mrs. Leyh, doffed his cap and enquired if he was at the right house.

"Yes of course, but would you give me a few minutes. I've only just arrived myself, and have no idea which rooms are which," replied Colette in her heavily accented English.

"No problem ma'am, take yer time, Arnold and me'll just start bringing things in and set them in this hall until yer ready. Right, Arnie?"

Arnie nodded mutely and went back to the horses.

Turning around in the hall, Colette saw elegant double doors to the left. This must be the parlor she thought, pushing the doors open. The ceiling was high, at least nine feet, and light flooded the room through the floor to ceiling window, even on this dull day. On the other side of the hall, she discovered a smaller room, darkly panelled, and to the rear was a large dining room. Following the noise coming from upstairs, Colette found the boys arguing, but turning away from their ongoing disagreement, she discovered a light filled master bedroom located directly over the parlor below. Through an adjoining door were dressing rooms and a green tiled bathroom with a massive tub. That, she thought, would be where she would shut herself in later and soak the cares of the day away; but for now it was back to the moving men. At least she now had some idea of where the furniture should go.

While she was upstairs, Arnie and his "guvner" had brought in most of the furniture and packing crates. Colette was not quite sure where to begin. How could Franz leave her like this, however urgent it was to secure the purchase of a factory in the East End of London? It was important for him to continue the corsetry business he'd owned in Belgium, but surely it could have waited a few hours. Left alone, she had to deal with the moving men, who were standing around waiting; the subsequent chaos; not to mention their boys Ernest and Robert, who were racing up and down the three floors of the house. In addition, the argument she'd heard earlier, about who was to have which bedroom, was starting to escalate.

"Will you boys stop running up and down the stairs? You are giving me a headache. Please just do something useful."

"What do you want us to do, Mama?"

Colette was losing patience. "Do you think your bags will get upstairs by themselves? I have to stay here to direct the moving men. Help out by taking them at least and, for pity's sake, do it quietly. My head is pounding."

Grabbing their bags, the boys hurtled upstairs, the

metal heels of their boots scraping over the marble, putting Colette's teeth on edge, and making her despair of any quiet in this house.

Flopping down on the nearest armchair sitting in the hall, Colette directed the moving men as best she could until there was a crash from outside. She jumped up as one of the men came through the door.

"Don't you worry ma'am, everything's fine, just a minor bump," he shouted.

Colette sank back into the chair, too tired to care. It had been an exhausting week. The journey from Spa across France to Le Havre, the rough Channel crossing, then a train ride to London, interspersed by nights in hotels, had all taken their toll, but only she seemed to find it intolerable. The boys were overly excited, Franz had gone off somewhere, and she just wanted to curl up and weep.

Just in time, someone came upstairs from the kitchen, introducing herself as Mrs. Scott, the cook. She was carrying a small tray with tea and buttered scones on it.

"I was thinking you might be in need of this, ma'am."

"Oh, you are so right, thank you. I think we will have to put it on the floor, though," replied Colette, looking around for a table.

"Hmmm, well, I think this packing case will serve as a table, if that's all right with you."

"I could drink that tea straight from the pot." Colette

laughed. "Perhaps you could bring another cup and join me?" she asked.

The cook was somewhat taken aback at the invitation. It was unthinkable for the help to take tea with the mistress, whatever the circumstances. Obviously, these were not the upper-crust employers she was used to working for.

"Thank you, ma'am, but I have duties in the kitchen to take care of. I took it upon myself to make a cold supper for you all, as I wasn't sure when you would be arriving, and I have something for the boys in the kitchen, if they are hungry now."

"Those boys are always hungry, and thank you so much for your thoughtfulness. I'll send them down right away."

Mrs. Scott left Colette to her tea, wondering what kind of household this would turn out to be. Hard to judge with foreigners with their funny ways.

Franz had bought the house on an earlier trip to London. It hadn't occurred to him that Colette should be consulted, but he had chosen well. Colette had only his description to go on, and a sheet of paper containing the room sizes, which wasn't terribly helpful when she was in Spa trying to decide which pieces of furniture to transport. Franz had bought her a map of London, and she had pored over it before they moved. Many of the historical sites she had only seen or read about in books were nearby and she was happy that Regent's Park was within walking distance. Now that she was actually here, she could see that opposite the house was a well-kept walled garden for the residents of Hanover Terrace to use. Sitting in the hallway looking at the imposing staircase to the upper floors, the house was much bigger and far grander than Colette would have chosen, but Franz was eager to take his place in both the English business and social scene. She just hoped they would fit in as he kept assuring her.

Colette had grown up in Spa, protected and pampered. She had lived in a private apartment at her parent's hotel in Spa, attending a good finishing school, with aspirations of going to an art college, but her parents wouldn't hear of it. She asked if she could learn the hotel trade, but her parents vetoed that as being both unladylike and beneath her. They were old fashioned and expected her to marry well, and as soon as possible. Colette had other ideas and rejected all the young men her parents introduced to her.

In a fit of pique and rebellion, she struck up a friendship with a short, older man called Franz Leyh. Her parents were not amused that she was involved with the swarthy, little man with few interests other than his factory. That it was a women's underwear factory was even worse. They were furious when, a few months later she announced she was marrying him and nothing, short of disowning her, would stop their determined daughter. Even that threat, which Colette knew to be an idle one,

would not change her mind. If Colette thought that marriage was her passport to freedom from her parents' rigid
control, she was sadly wrong.

Franz was as old fashioned as her parents, but two
babies born just a year apart kept Colette busy, and she
put thoughts of working anywhere but in the home out of
her mind. Her parents came around, relieved that their
only daughter had settled down and they adored their
grandchildren. Franz was proving to be a good provider
and their daughter seemed content to live in Franz's small
house not far from the hotel.

Even though Colette had railed against her parents in
the past, she was devastated when, just a few short years
later, they died within weeks of each other in one of the
influenza epidemics that scourged Europe nearly every
winter. With their death, Colette lost all interest in the hotel and she agreed with Franz that they should sell it. As
the only child and heir, she had a significant inheritance,
but as was expected, she passed the money from the sale
to Franz to invest. With Colette's agreement, he used the
funds to expand his foundation garment business, *Solei-
Soie,* making it into the great success it was. With the
help of his chief designer, the elderly Mme. Mireille, orders came from Paris, London, even New York. The future had looked so rosy. Now they were strangers in England, having to make a new life for themselves.

Franz returned home late, eager to tell Colette about
the property he had negotiated for in the East End of

London. "It will do just fine. It's easily converted once the machines arrive, and there's a lot of girls and women wanting work," he told her excitedly. "I saw an underground railway station nearby. Did you ever hear of such a thing? That will get me there and back home quickly, so I think it will be ideal," he rattled off.

"Isn't the East End a very rough part of the city?" Colette asked. "What about that Jack the Ripper? They never caught him you know. Will you be safe coming and going there?

The East End was indeed a tough neighborhood, full of alleys and narrow streets leading from the St. Katharine's Dock with it's dark, brooding warehouses blocking out the sunlight. Thick fog often shrouded the streets making anyone unlucky enough to be out easy prey for pickpockets and thugs. The long, straight streets with two up, two down terraced houses were overcrowded, as refugees from the Irish potato famine had poured in looking for work on the docks. Russians, Poles and Jews soon joined them, escaping from Europe, just as the Leyh's had, all looking for safety from the pogroms. Unlike the Leyh's, the immigrants settling in the East End were poverty stricken, taking whatever accommodation they could find. Many of the Europeans were skilled workers and, with what little funds they had, set up small workshops where their own could find employment. Many of the unskilled, found work on market stalls, or if they were lucky, as porters at Billingsgate, where the an-

glers sold the night's fish catch at first light. With the in-
flux of immigrants, came more public houses and broth-
els. The East End became synonymous with drunkenness,
fights, and immoral behavior. Franz, ever the optimist,
tried to reassure his wife.

"Yes it's a rough neighborhood, but there's good and
bad in all places, my dear, but mostly the East Enders are
an honest lot, I'm told. Besides where would I find my
work force? I don't think the ladies of Mayfair would be
keen to become seamstresses." He laughed. "Don't worry
so much my dear, I'm sure Jack the Ripper must be long
dead by now."

Anxious to get the factory running as soon as possible, Franz needed to advertise the opportunity for the area's much-needed employment. Taking a hansom cab to
Fleet Street, knowing this being the hub of the newspaper
world, he felt sure someone in the business would know
where he could have flyers printed.

He needed to advertise for staff, and a poster protected by glass and hung on the factory gates should work, as
it was a busy street.

A few flyers posted in small shop windows nearby
should also find him the help he wanted. Directed to a
print shop not far from Fleet Street, he had the flyers and
a large poster made up, showing the need for seamstresses, cleaners, and maintenance personnel—anyone and
everyone that would get his factory ready for operation.

Back at the factory, he wired the poster to the gate

and waited inside the building. It wasn't long before the curious were knocking on the door.

Over the next few weeks, the old, dingy building transformed. On opening day, a line of shabbily dressed women stood waiting for the gates to open.

Franz had hand-picked them himself, taking those with experience, but also young women looking to start work and learn the trade from the older women.

As they filed in, they stood awkwardly looking around.

Franz, smiling broadly with his son Ernest at his side, asked them to stand for a moment as he explained what their duties would be. A few of the older women mumbled the likes of "Going to teach his mother how to suck eggs then," thinking they had all the experience they needed.

"Ladies, welcome to *Soleil Soie*. You have before you the latest in sewing equipment, and I think you will agree, the best of working conditions. However, before you start, I must explain that the fabrics you will handle need a most delicate touch, and absolute cleanliness is essential. In that regard, you will find in the…er…*toilette* the gentlest of soaps and lotions. Please use the lotions after work, not before—we can't have any oil transferring to the fabric."

"Fancy that—lotions, what next?" was heard from several women, as they glanced down at their work-worn hands.

"Lotions will soften your hands, so they do not snag the fabrics," Franz answered somewhat curtly. "You will not have worked on such fine fabrics before, I'm sure. We use French silk, and Brussels lace. Does anyone have a problem with that?"

Not a whisper was heard, but several pairs of eyebrows were raised, as the women looked at one another.

"In addition, we will supply a white apron, to be washed every week. Anyone appearing with a soiled apron will not be allowed to work until you arrive with a clean one."

A lot of muttering was heard then. For some, laundry facilities were meager and drying, even worse. The long wash lines hanging across the streets often took days to dry, and ended up smutty from the coal fire smoke blowing from the chimneys.

One woman, bolder than the rest took this up with Franz. "Mr. Leyh, how will we get the aprons clean? You've seen the wash lines."

Franz had to think. Washing had not been a problem in the clean air of Spa. "Very well, you will leave the aprons here each night, and, at the end of the week, I will get them laundered." The muttering rose to a cheer. "Now, ladies, to work!"

Franz happily went off to his factory each morning, taking the underground train. The lift taking him down to the platform, ground its way agonizingly slowly, sinking deeper and deeper on its creaking chains. As many times as he took the lift, he was always relieved once he felt the bump at the platform level. Advertisements papered onto the walls gave some relief to the gloomy tunnel that disappeared into darkness. The train arrived by an electric rail, and warning signs were posted to stay away from the edge and not to cross the tracks or risk electrocution. The air was hot and thick but Franz persisted. It was a most convenient means of transport.

As the weeks passed Franz, Frank as his English colleagues called him, was rarely home. The grim exterior of the factory now boasted an elegant sign *Soleil Soie,* generally mispronounced by the workers as *Solly Soy.* Once the sewing machines had arrived, he had been busy overseeing their installation, training staff, even hiring a tea lady, a job he'd not come across in Spa. It seemed the women could not work without liberal cups of tea. Still, that was a small price to pay if the factory functioned efficiently.

He had been appalled at working conditions in the area and even more so by the living conditions. His factory was clean, and light filled the workroom from the new electric lights strung across the ceiling. Conditions here were good, the hours and wages fair, and soon the factory was a model of modern efficiency. Franz, determined to lead by example, hoped other employers would follow suit, but his standards seemed to cause resentment, even open hostility from other factory owners when they lost staff to him. Women were eager to work for Franz, especially as he spoke several of the immigrant languages when he stopped to speak with them on the factory floor.

CHAPTER 2

Settling In

Colette, feeling overwhelmed at times, had organized the house into some sort of order. Although she had lived in a hotel most of her life, she was unused to dealing with the staff. Her parents' apartment was mysteriously cleaned, linens changed, clothes laundered, and meals provided by an invisible force, which came and went about their duties, and she hardly ever saw them. She had baulked at Mrs. Scott's suggestion of hiring a butler and housekeeper, but it soon became apparent that if she didn't want to deal with all the household matters herself, they would have to be engaged.

"Madam, it's not my place to hire staff, and as Mr.

Leyh is otherwise occupied, you will have to, but I will help if you need me."

"Mrs. Scott, I can't do this without you. I haven't any idea how to go about even finding applicants. Where do I start?"

"Well, I can contact the previous owner's agency and they will send us a list of possibilities, and then you must select the ones you wish to interview."

"I'm going to leave it to you, Mrs. Scott, if you don't mind. You know the sort of people we need," replied Colette, who was once again feeling out of her depth.

"Well, madam, I'm happy to oblige in any way I can and I'll get onto it right away. We can't go on without adequate help, can we?"

"You're right, but I don't want any live in staff."

Mrs. Scott's eyebrows rose, but she held her tongue. What new nonsense was *this*? "Do you not want a lady's maid madam?"

"No, oh I don't know," Colette wailed. "Hire whomever you think, and we'll have to get used to it. Though what Mr. Leyh will think of all the intrusion and expense, I don't know."

Good as her word, Mrs. Scott contacted the agency and interviewed the applicants. It didn't take long before the house had a basic complement of staff, although Franz loudly rejected the idea of his having a man to dress him.

Once the house was functioning, it was time to find a

school for the boys. Franz had decided on Westminster School, it being one of the best, and the boys could attend as day students as it was nearby. Being somewhat paranoid about his Jewish roots, because of what had happened in Spa, he insisted that the family was now Church of England, whatever that was. Colette was to say they had been Lutheran in Belgium, as having no specific religion would not bode well for the boys' acceptance into a Christian school. Franz could easily give up his heritage, but she hated lying to the school, to herself, and to the boys. Still, they, at least, were too young to understand or care.

Colette had no idea about the class system in England, or that a child registered in a "good" school at birth, so when she arrived at the school she was unprepared for the cool reception she received. Westminster was a choir school attached to the magnificent Westminster Abbey and Franz, wanting the boys to have a first rate education, assured her that this was the *best* school. As he had the where withal to pay, he didn't see any problem. The boys were fluent in English, having had an English governess at home in Spa, so at least that wasn't an issue and a religious school might calm them down a bit.

Without Franz, the three of them sat nervously waiting in the foyer, the boys quiet for a change, overwhelmed by the size and grandeur of the building. Eventually, a pleasant young man appeared to take them on a tour and answer any questions they might have. When a column of young boys clad in choir gowns rushed down the hallway and disappeared into the Abbey, the boys asked their mother, thankfully in French, if they too would have to wear those "dresses." If they thought the young man wouldn't understand, they were mistaken, as he replied kindly in French that they were choir gowns, and only worn in the Abbey. The school supplied a suitable uniform *with trousers,* worn most of the time. Colette was embarrassed, but the young man was reassuring and said that that was often the reaction of new boys. At the end of one hallway, graced with dark portraits of previous headmasters, their guide knocked on the door and said they would now meet the current headmaster.

The young man grinned. "Don't be nervous, he doesn't bite."

The boys laughed, but the joke was lost on Colette, who almost trembled when a deep voice invited them to enter. Behind a huge oak desk, piled high with music sheets sat a very small man whose voice belied his size. The interview was mercifully short and, when asked if the boys sang, Colette could at least answer truthfully that they both had fine voices. It seemed that acceptance hinged on voice quality, rather than academics. Moving to a piano across the room, the headmaster put the giggling boys to a voice test. After a short discussion on religion, and the headmaster looking down his boney nose at Colette regarding their ignorance of Church of England teachings, both boys were accepted. The interview with the headmaster had been an ordeal for Collette, as her English was stilted at best, and annoyingly Franz was once again away on business at the time.

Breathing a sigh of relief in the fresh air outside, the boys, having been confined and quiet for so long, started to badger Colette.

"Mama, can we go to the Natural History Museum now?" they wanted to know.

Colette had more or less promised them that if all went well at the school, she would take them. "Boys, I am too tired after that trial with the headmaster, but we will go tomorrow, I promise. You can play in the square for a while before supper if you like, but you must change first."

The boys were none too happy. The park was a poor substitute for the dinosaurs in the museum, but once home and changed into old clothes, they charged out into the park to burn off some energy running around and climbing trees, much to the annoyance of elderly neighbors expecting a peaceful afternoon.

Colette was glad to see them out of the house, ready to have a few minutes to herself, and a large sherry to revive her.

With the household functioning, and the boys' education settled, she realized how lonely life in London was. If only she had some female company. It was proving harder to break into English society than Colette had ever imagined. In Spa, there had been many old school friends for tea parties, picnics, and dinners. Skiing and skating in winter kept her fit, and the *après* ski initiated new friendships. How did one make friends here in haughty Mayfair? Walking the garden across the road made only nodding acquaintances. The neighbors of Hanover Terrace were Lady This and Lord That, unwilling to extend invitations to the newcomers who were in trade, and obviously not of their class. Uniformed nannies with babies were above the status of household staff, but not the sort of women one asked to tea—besides, they'd never agree.

Franz had more success in making acquaintances, if not actual friends. Because he was "in trade," the upper classes were beyond his aspirations, but his business colleagues had wives who were interested to meet Franz's wife, and even more so to be invited to the Mayfair house.

Eventually, dinner invitations were accepted and reciprocated, and Colette began to feel more at home in England. Mrs. Scott had approved the household staff, and although it was taking time for Colette to feel comfortable with them, especially the housekeeper and butler, she had to agree, it was much easier than trying to deal with everything herself. As her English improved, she became more confident, and, with the help of her newly found women friends, began exploring London.

The factory was up and running and making a profit, despite Franz's continued annoyance at the rapid change in fashions which necessitated new and innovative designs in corsetry. His expertise ran more to the mechanics of corsetry, and he was ill prepared for the changes. A new designer had to be found, and quickly. Surely, someone would have the necessary knowledge and flair that his designer in Spa had. After weeks of advertising, and interviewing, no one suitable came forward. In frustration, he wrote to his old designer in Spa, asking her if she knew of anyone who might be interested in joining him.

Sylvie Mireille now retired, was living quietly in Spa. She knew that the person Franz was looking for would be hard to find. She took stock of her own life—retirement was not very fulfilling. She had enough money for the basics, but her days were long. Working all her life, she had few friends, and the thought of endless afternoon teas and gossip had filled her with dread. She was still a vibrant woman, she told herself. Should she offer to take up the position in London herself? As she sat mulling over her options, the doorbell to her apartment building rang. She could hardly believe her ears when she heard Franz asking if she was at home.

"Franz, come up, come up" she cried as she pressed the front door release.

"No wonder you look so well," Franz said, seeing her at her door, and he puffing from the exertion of walking up the three floors to her suite.

"And you are sadly not so fit. Do you not get any exercise in that grand city you live in?" she chided him. "What are you doing here? I wrote and told you I didn't know of anyone suitable. Didn't you get my letter?"

"Yes, I did, and I'm desperate, Sylvie. I've come to ask you to come back with me. I really need your expertise and flair."

Sylvie smiled to herself as she turned to the kitchen to make Franz a cup of coffee. Theirs was an old relationship. They knew each other so well, but she was not going to make this too easy for him.

"Well, I'm flattered of course, but I'm settled here. I'm retired for heaven's sake!"

"Sylvie, don't make me beg," Franz said, smiling. He knew the game they were playing.

"Very well, I'll come for a while, but I'm not sure I will stay."

"I'll organize and pay for everything it takes to get you to London" Franz assured her.

She laughed. "You most certainly will! I'll be there in a week. Now let's have that coffee to seal the deal."

When Franz told Collette he'd persuaded her old friend Sylvie out of retirement in Belgium to assist in designing the intimate items, she was overjoyed. She knew he had worried himself sick about the lack of a creative assistant. As his chief designer in Spa, Sylvie knew the business so well that Franz could rely on her more and more in the future. He was well aware of the cat and mouse game Sylvie had played with him in Spa. Once in England, she would stay as long as she could work, he knew that. Sylvie was far more than an employee. She was a link to Colette's past and someone with whom to enjoy spending time.

When she arrived somewhat later than the week she had estimated, she stayed at the Hanover Terrace residence, but soon asked Colette to help her find a small house or an apartment. Much as Sylvie liked the boys, it was time to move, possibly because, as a single woman of mature years, she found the noisy chaos of them too much to bear, but of course, she would never have said so.

Colette enjoyed helping her find the perfect place, which turned out to be a small mews cottage just around the corner from Hanover Terrace. Sylvie was not only a designer, but also a shrewd businesswoman. She had done her homework and had negotiated the purchase of the cottage for less than the asking price. Once it was in Sylvie's possession, the two women scoured the West End for furnishings to make it a warm and homely place.

"Do you know, I have never owned a property before," Sylvie exclaimed as they had tea in her parlor after a marathon-shopping spree.

"Then this is doubly exciting" replied Colette. "I must admit finding the right things for your home is much nicer than setting up the house in Hanover Terrace. It's a lovely house but I still feel it's not mine, what with Franz buying without my even seeing it," she said wistfully. Colette was still finding the grandeur of the place intimidating, preferring this little cottage so much more.

"Then I shall not feel guilty in asking you to come with me to Liberty's store. I still need to buy materials for curtains for this room, also a new rug for the dining room, and I'm told that is the best shop for such things. Also the window boxes, I need plants—lots of plants— and a painter, the front is a little shabby…"

"Wonderful, shall we start on Saturday?" Colette enthused. "I know Franz keeps you busy throughout the week. I'll ask Mrs. Scott about finding a painter and plants—she'll know, or if she doesn't she'll find out. She's such a treasure. I'm so lucky to have her."

The following weekend, Colette took a hansom cab to Sylvie's house, finding her already in coat and hat, eager to go shopping.

"You haven't seen much of London since you arrived, have you?" remarked Colette, "so, I'm taking you on a little tour."

The cab took them past all the major sites and around the big parks now in full bloom.

Sylvie was entranced. "It's so beautiful. I had no idea!" she gushed.

"Well, this part is, but I'm afraid the factory is in quite a poor area, I understand. I don't want you traveling to and from there alone, so I've asked Franz to accompany you in the morning and bring you home at night. He takes the dreadful Underground. I hope you won't be afraid of it. If for any reason he can't go with you, or you find the train intolerable, he's to call you a cab," Colette declared.

"That seems a little over protective, and I've yet to see this Underground, but I do understand and thank you most sincerely. Now to business, where is this Liberty's shop?"

CHAPTER 3

Bicycles

Whenever Franz had time, which wasn't often, he would take the boys to Regents Park, where they rode their bicycles. As Ernest and Robert rode up and down in front of him, Franz couldn't help but think about the bicycles themselves and how they could be improved upon. He began taking a sketching pad on their afternoons at the park. After designing corsets, bicycles should be no problem!

Their usual route took them through the zoo. The boys insisted and never grew tired of seeing the animals. They still had to experience a winter in London, which would be so different from Spa. Franz hoped they wouldn't fret about being unable to ski and skate. He hoped winter would be cold enough to skate on the park ponds. School was taking up much of their time, but they had boundless energy. He would have to get them into some sort of winter sport or they'd drive their mother insane during the winter months.

After watching the boys bouncing over the cobbled path around the fountain, he called out to them. "Boys come here a moment, I need you."

"What is it, Papa?"

"Let me have a go on your bicycle" he said, grabbing the handles of Robert's bicycle and swinging his leg awkwardly over it.

"You're too big, Papa," they cried, but, to the boys' amusement, he made a wobbly circuit round the same fountain.

"Just as I thought" he muttered. Once seated on the bench, he began sketching.

"Look, what do you think about this?" he asked, showing the sketch to them.

The two lads looked at the peculiar sketch on the pad, then at each other.

"It's great, Papa—what is it?" asked Robert.

"It's a saddle with springs of course."

"What do the springs do?" Ernest asked.

"They will revolutionize bicycle riding by making it comfortable over rough roads and maybe make us a lot of money!" their father replied excitedly.

"My dear, I want to tell you about my new business

venture," Franz said, opening the dinner conversation a few weeks later.

"Does it have anything to do with bicycles, Franz? You've been obsessed with them for weeks."

"Yes, it does. Do you recall I had a meeting with a Mr. Robinson?" he continued.

"You have so many appointments, I can't say I do," she replied distractedly as she tried to settle the boys to behave at the table.

"Well, George Robinson is a successful bicycle manufacturer, and he's interested in my designs and wants to buy them. I told him I was only interested in a partnership, though. It was a struggle, but he finally agreed."

Colette was under no illusion that Franz would do exactly what he wanted, but she was worried about how he would run two companies at once. He was rarely home as it was, and the boys needed more attention from their father now that they were getting older.

"You must do what you feel is best, but please don't exhaust yourself. Remember you had that chest infection last winter, and I really don't think you are fully recovered from it," she reminded him.

Franz and George became trusted friends and partners. Business was booming, but George was even more restless than Franz.

He was developing a passion for the motor car, spending time gleaning information about the industry from the motor factories in Europe and America. Coming back from one of his trips, he was eager to speak to Franz, who he called Frankie.

"Frankie, what do you think about expanding into motor cars? I think they are the future and we should be at the forefront of this exciting innovation, don't you?"

George continued his research into the motor car until November, two years later. London was taking on its familiar fog shrouded damp days, and dark early nights. Franz came home obviously with something on his mind.

"Whatever is troubling you dearest," asked Colette.

"I have a decision to make which will affect our family," he said dourly.

"Whatever is it? You're frightening me, Franz," she cried.

"Oh, my dear, I'm sorry if I upsetting you. It's just that George is keen to take the business into manufacturing motor cars, and I feel it would be overtaxing our financial position, to an extent that I could not cover, should things go wrong. For the past two years, he's been researching the industry, now he's looking for financing as he's ready to go ahead."

Franz was obviously in turmoil.

"I really think I will have to sever my partnership with George. I'm not sure the motor car has as big a future for personal motoring as he seems to think. They are far too expensive to build for most of the population to buy," he said ruefully.

A few days later George Robinson and his wife came

to dinner. After dining, George and Franz disappeared into the study to discuss their respective futures over their usual brandy and cigars.

Colette did not particularly like George's wife, but she was duty bound to entertain her while the men talked.

"George." Franz sighed. "George, it gives me great pain to have to ask you to sever our partnership, but I can't get involved in the motor car expansion that you want to pursue."

"I'm sorry to hear that, Frankie, but it's your decision. We've discussed the implications before and I know you're not comfortable with all it entails. As an alternative, perhaps you might be interested in buying my share of Robinson's Bicycles. I could do with a cash injection to go ahead with my plans, and there will always be a need for bicycles you know."

"That's rather what I had in mind, George, and if we can come to terms, that's what we will do," replied Franz.

"We've had a good run together, Frank, and I will always value your friendship. Before I leave bicycle manufacture, show me your latest designs. Knowing you, I'm sure you have a number of innovations that will keep the company going well into the future."

Franz breathed a sigh of relief. George had taken the news well, and they would remain friends and confidants, if no longer partners. After working out the details, Franz bought George's share of the bicycle business and, with their respective solicitors on hand, signed the relevant documents, and sealed them with a handshake. As ever, Franz relished a new challenge. Now the company was his alone. He had the sole authority to bring his new designs to life.

CHAPTER 4

Paris

The years were passing by quickly. The boys were about to leave school, having sat their matriculation exams. Neither was keen to pursue a university education as, from their exam results, it was obvious neither was particularly academic. Ernest was taking an interest in accounting, spending time poring over the books of both factories with the accountant. Robert was, to his father's dismay, more interested in the club life of London and was the cause of many disagreements between his parents.

Franz finally seemed content. He still worked long hours in the bicycle factory, orders coming in for the latest model as soon as they could be built. The corset factory, *Soleil Soie,* was running itself almost without him, due to the diligence of a new manager and Sylvie Mireille, who worked with the energy of a woman half her age. She was often a guest at the house, as she and Colette enjoyed gossiping about their old social life in Belgium.

At one of their regular dinners together, Sylvie brought up the subject of having Colette more involved in *Soleil Soie.* She knew that Colette was restless now that the boys were growing, and with her keen mind and design sense, she ought to be more active in the business.

"Franz, I have been thinking—"

Franz laughed. "Sylvie, that usually means trouble."

Keeping the tone of conversation light she continued. "Franz, I am getting on in years, and I need a younger woman's perspective on design and construction. I was thinking that Colette should help me. She's certainly a lot younger and is interested in the upcoming trends. I'd like her to accompany me to Paris on my annual trip. She would be a great asset if you would let her go."

"Strange you should mention that, Sylvie. I was thinking only the other day about your trip coming up, but I am concerned about either of you traveling to Europe in these uncertain times."

"Oh, tosh! You are such a worrier, Franz. We will only be gone for a week or so, what could possibly happen?" she replied.

"I know I worry, but all right, a week, no more, and immediately—that is, if you want to go, Colette?"

Colette was thrilled. It had been so long since she had visited Paris. Pity it would only be a week. It would have been nice to go on to Spa and see her old friends.

"I'll begin packing at once," she said excitedly.

The two of them set off on their trip three days later. Sylvie, far from needing help because of her age, was as excited as Colette. There were no sleeping compartments on the paddle steamer, but a comfortable salon below deck offered a rather too close a view of the waves. Sitting away from the windows, the two women spent the time discussing the couture houses they would visit. It was important to see the new clothing designs to envisage the corsetry that went underneath and its' construction. The Channel was mercifully calm, and, after an uneventful crossing, both women went up on deck to catch their first glimpse of the French coast.

It was good to be on land once again, and Colette and Sylvie lost no time in getting a train to Paris. Once settled in their hotel, Sylvie set about retrieving their tickets to three couture showings.

The next day when the two women entered the elegant salon of Monsieur LeBlanc, the hosts enthusiastically greeted Sylvie. Colette was surprised to see what a rapport she had with these icons of fashion.

There was more to Mme. Mireille than was widely known.

"How do you know these people so well, Sylvie?"

"Ah, I have had connections for many years and—

for your ears only—I was the mistress of one of them in my youth."

Colette's eyes widened "Which one?" she asked breathlessly."

"Oh, it's so long ago, and I don't think his wife would want to hear of it now," Sylvie replied coyly. "Let's just watch the show, and do make lots of notes, my dear."

Colette had never been to a couture fashion show. Invitations were usually reserved for the rich and famous, sometimes the infamous!

As they took their seats, she looked around in awe. There was no sign here of the austerity that most of Europe was enduring. The salon itself was luxurious with velvet drapery and little gold painted chairs that were elegant if uncomfortable.

They sat a few rows from the front but would still have a good view of the models as they passed along the raised pathway which Sylvie informed her was called a *cat walk*.

A wave of elegantly gowned women finally took the front row seats.

"Do you know any of these women, Sylvie?" Colette whispered.

"Well, not personally, but that is one of the Rothschild sisters," she said, pointing to a tall, thin woman clad in furs. "And the woman coming in now is Maud Allan, the actress. She caused a sensation when rumours spread that she appeared completely naked under her flimsy costume for her *Dance of Salomé*."

Colette's jaw dropped. "You know so much about life Sylvie. I feel as if I have been wrapped in a bubble all of mine!"

"Well you have led a sheltered upbringing, but now enough name dropping, my dear, let's enjoy the show."

Sylvie was right about the change in styles. The heavily boned *S* corset was gone. Waistlines rose to just under the bust, but even the more natural styles still required support.

"I am so glad to see a more normal form, but Franz is going to have a fit. We will have to completely re-design all our lines," Sylvie remarked.

Their few days in Paris flew by and soon they were getting ready to return to London. Before they left, the two women walked the length of the Champs Elise, stopping to look in the boutique windows at the latest fashions, drinking coffee in the cafes, and eating the croissants for which the French patisseries were so famous.

"Sylvie, it is so good to talk in French again," Colette remarked. "English is so difficult and I miss having an easy conversation."

"Your English is very good now, but I know what you mean. Some things just don't sound right when we have to translate all the time. Let's take one last ride to the left bank and look at the artists' work," Sylvie suggested. "Maybe you will find a painting to go over your drawing room mantle."

"What a good idea. I have never found anything in the London galleries that I think Franz will like."

"Oh, phooey to what Franz likes. Find something that says, *take me home*, buy it, hang it, and tell Franz how wonderful it is and such a bargain!"

"Oh, Sylvie, I do love being with you. You're so wicked."

The next day, gathering up far more than they had arrived with, Sylvie and Colette ate a breakfast of croissants and confiture, washed down with incredibly strong coffee.

When they had finished and paid the bill, they took a lingering stroll through the Bois du Boulogne and, upon their return to the hotel, waited while the porter brought out their bags and piled them into a hansom cab to take them to the Gare du Nord.

The station was busy as only a Paris station could be. The two women drank in the shouting and gesturing at which Parisians excelled. Even the smell of the rancid Gauloise cigarettes would be something they'd consign to their memories of the trip.

Finding a porter was a challenge, but the cab driver finally came back with, not one, but two burly men who set to work getting their bags and packages onto the train.

Their carriage was full of mothers, tired from a morning of shopping in Paris and left their ill-behaved

children to their nannies or tried to quiet them themselves.

"Why are French children so badly behaved, I wonder," Colette whispered to Sylvie.

"Ah, it is preferable to the insufferable English way
of *seeing but not hearing* their children," Sylvie replied
tartly.

"I used to despair of Robert and Ernest's behavior,
but now I wish they were little children again, especially
Robert. He's such a trial to his father." Colette sighed. "I
try to keep it from Franz, to spare myself the unpleasantness, but Robert goes out drinking, and I'm sure he's
gambling with his wastrel friends."

"Oh, Colette, all children are a trial to their parents.
I'm sure he will mature and become as responsible as
Ernest eventually."

It wasn't long before the train chugged out of the station and gained speed across the French countryside,
making several stops before arriving at Le Havre where
the steamer would take them back across the English
Channel.

The last time she had made this journey, Colette was
apprehensive about leaving all that was familiar to her to
live in a foreign land. This time she wasn't worried and
was looking forward to telling Franz and the boys all
about her time in Paris.

A fine rain was falling as they arrived at the Le Havre docks, and once they had seen the bags safely on

board, the two women wasted no time in getting to the salon.

The weather took a turn for the worse and, once outside the harbour, the Channel became quite rough. Colette felt fine, but Sylvie began to feel seasick. Lunch for her was out of the question, so Colette went to the dining room without her. She found herself alone at her table, with few people around, so she ordered her lunch quickly and, after eating, tried to take a cup of tea back to Sylvie, but the rocking of the ship slopped more into the saucer than remained in the cup.

Hours later, it was evening by the time the boat docked at Dover. Colette had her hands full supporting Sylvie who was still feeling unwell. Wishing they hadn't bought quite so much, with all the loading and unloading, she was happy to find a porter. Instead of going to the booking hall for train tickets, she decided to take Sylvie to the station hotel for the night, to recuperate before tackling the next journey. The hotel concierge helped Colette send a telegram to Franz, telling him of their delay, knowing he would be frantic until assured they were safe.

The following morning, they were up early to catch the first train. An elderly porter struggled with their luggage across the street to the station and, being quite helpful, earned a substantial tip, as Colette was so relieved to finally board the train to London.

Once aboard, Sylvie was feeling somewhat better and the color returned to her cheeks. She was quiet on the journey, but just before the train pulled into London, she turned to Colette. "I wish Franz would allow you to work with me."

"I'd like that too, but Franz is so old fashioned and, even though he hires mostly women, I don't think that will ever happen. But I have enjoyed this trip, and you can always consult with me if you need to," Colette replied.

CHAPTER 5

Storm Clouds

F ranz," Colette said at the breakfast table. "Franz, look at me, I'm speaking to you. What is so interesting in the newspaper, that you let your breakfast get cold? Robert, Ernest, please eat up and get ready. Franz!"

"Cherie, things are getting very difficult in Europe." he replied, frowning. "I do believe we will be drawn into a war against Germany. If the Kaiser continues his aggression, Britain will have no option."

Colette went pale. "Another war, the Boer War wasn't so very long ago," she whispered. While Colette was an intelligent woman, she rarely took an interest in current affairs, especially those abroad. She had had a fleeting interest in the suffrage movement, but Franz would not have tolerated any involvement on her part.

"Just be grateful we are here in England, Colette. The Germans will never get across the Channel," he reassured her.

The storm clouds gathered momentum. With the assassination of Franz Ferdinand of Austria, European states began forming alliances. Russia mobilized against Austria-Hungary, who had declared war on Serbia. Through July and August, Germany forced its way through Luxembourg, declaring war on France, and finally Belgium. On August 4, 1914, Britain declared war against Germany. The nightmare was about to begin.

It wasn't long after war had been declared that Franz was summoned to a government office in Central London. He learned that the army needed uniforms, and his bicycle factory was being expropriated to begin manufacturing them.

"Mr. Leyh, am I talking to a patriotic man?" asked the officer in a colonel's uniform from behind his desk.

"But of course, sir. I have been resident in Britain for many years, and what is happening in my native country, Belgium is an outrage," Franz replied.

"Good, this country needs you and your factory to make uniforms for our fighting men," the colonel continued. "I understand you have knowledge of tailoring?"

"My factory is at your disposal, sir. My workers will be honored to help the war effort," replied Franz. "But surely my other factory would be more suitable as it is at least set up for clothing manufacture."

"No, sir, we feel the factory we have chosen is better suited for distribution," the colonel retorted. He was not used to having his decisions questioned.

Franz shrugged his shoulders. It made no sense to him, but he had no option but to comply.

There was only a short time to dismantle, remove, and find storage for the existing machinery in the plant. Hardly had the last piece been removed when bales of heavy woollen material arrived at the east end factory, along with industrial sewing machines, a pattern cutter, and several instructors to teach the newly hired girls and women how to construct army greatcoats. A number of the male employees stayed on, mostly older men who grumbled at having to learn a new trade at their age! Many of the younger lads, eager for adventure, had already rushed off to join the army.

Back at Hanover Terrace, Franz was mulling over the implications of having his factory taken over by the military.

"They are paying, aren't they? The military I mean," asked Colette. "We're not expected to pay the girls ourselves, are we?"

"No, no, my dear, but we can't expect to make a profit on the war effort, can we? We'll probably have to rely on just the income from *Soleil Soie* for the time being," Franz replied. "I must speak to Ernest. He has a

flare for accounting. We will make sense of it together,"
he reassured her.

Colette had little business sense, but she had the
thought, though unvoiced, that maybe women wouldn't
want so many corsets in a war. Things were going to get
very difficult unless they made concessions to the war
effort.

Colette rarely made comments regarding the business, but she felt compelled to mention an idea she had.
She was right in thinking that a woman's priority in wartime wasn't to buy many new corsets. Just as well, as it
was becoming increasingly difficult for Franz to obtain
the metal stays now, with every scrap of metal needed for
armaments.

There was still a small, continuous demand, and the
factory kept the wolf from the Hanover Terrace door but
the family's income was perilously low.

That night over dinner with Franz and the boys, she
nervously brought up her idea. "Franz, I know I don't
know much about business, but wouldn't it be a good
idea to use *Solei Soie* to make working clothes for women
now that so many are doing men's work?"

Franz's spoon stopped in mid-air. "Colette, you
know, you may be onto something. We need an alternative source of income and what you suggest has merit. I
think we should look into it, don't you, boys? My dear,
thank you, we will give it some thought," he replied.

Colette wasn't finished. "I have a few sketches that

might work. I showed them to Sylvie and she was very complimentary."

"I never realized you were interested in the business, Mama," said Ernest.

"I don't think I was before, but as you know, I've always enjoyed sketching, and to draw something useful…well, I just thought I'd try…for the war effort."

"Mama, could you show us the sketches," asked Robert.

"Of course, we will look at them after dinner," she replied happily.

The four of them spent several hours that night, examining the sketches and discussing the styles. Colette had been quite prolific and had designs for bus drivers, factory workers, even lamplighters, many of them with a most controversial item—trousers!

It wasn't long before space was allocated in the factory, heavier sewing machines brought in, and, within weeks, fabric ordered and delivered. Not the best quality and nothing like the fine fabrics the seamstresses were used to, but serviceable and wearable for the difficult, and often harsh environments women now found themselves in.

Later that year, Franz was called to the same government office he had visited before. This time they wanted the corset factory for the manufacture of munitions. This would prove a deep financial blow to the family.

"Sir, I know the need is great, but my factory is situated in the east end, near the docks. Surely, it would be too dangerous for the residents. The docks are a continual target for zeppelins and even aircraft bombers," Franz countered, in a desperate attempt to keep some income for the family.

"That's as may be, but it's because the factory is near the docks that we need it. Don't want to have to transport dangerous cargo too far through the streets," replied the officer.

Franz's objections were simply swept aside.

Solei Soie would have to relocate, time was of the essence as there were orders outstanding, and the family desperately needed the income. That evening the family and Sylvie gathered around the dinner table and Franz began.

"Family, I have to tell you that the *Solei Soie* will have to move to a new location, as we are being taken over for munitions manufacture. Sylvie and Colette gasped and looked at each other as he continued. "Ernest and I will oversee the removal of our equipment and the conversion to a munitions plant. Robert, you will have to look after the move once we have a new location," Franz said, hoping that Robert would show some initiative, given this responsibility. "Start looking for premises, Robert, not too far away as I'd like to keep the girls we have, now that they are proficient in our lines. Also it should be somewhat larger than our current premises, as I want to expand the work wear production." He turned to his other son. "Ernest, you and I will have to work with the war department. They want to get into the factory very soon."

"What can I do?" Colette asked, not wishing to be left out.

"Yes, yes, Colette, you will work with Sylvie once the new site is found. I hate to put too much on you, but I really will need your help to get things up and running again," Franz replied.

Colette almost smiled despite the awful news. Finally she would be able to work—and with Franz's blessing.

Once the sewing machines were removed, the munitions equipment coming in didn't overly tax Franz and Ernest. The war office organized almost everything with military precision and a substantial work force. Heavy machinery along with chemicals and explosives trucked in. There were guards on the gate, and all the newly hired workers had to show their identity badges. For the time being, Ernest acted as controller and bookkeeper, hiring as many staff as needed. Because the war ministry paid top wages for munitions workers, girls flooded the recruitment office, eager to earn a better salary.

Finding a new site for the *Solei Soie* factory in the East end was proving a challenge for Robert. Most of the properties he found were in deplorable condition, or unsuitable in one way or another. He was anxious to find a place and show his father that he was reliable and could be trusted to do what was required of him. Finally, he found a warehouse that, with a lot of cleaning, but little renovation could be fitted out in short order. For the girls not wanting to work in munitions, preferring to follow *Solei Soie* to its new location, Robert cajoled some of them finding themselves temporarily unemployed, to clean and refurbish the new premises. Handsome and charming, he could almost persuade birds from the trees. Soon the girls, giggling and clad in overalls, were putting up shelves for storing the fabric, moving the equipment, and finally getting the sewing machines that had been piled in one corner, to the workbenches.

Impressed by Robert's enthusiasm and hard work, Colette was on hand to keep an eye on him. In addition, she had to watch the girls, as more than one of them had set her sights on the younger son of the family, and Robert did little to discourage them.

"Oi, Mr. Leyh, give us an 'and with this crate," simpered one girl, sidling up to him.

Colette, resorting to French, chastised him soundly for being over friendly with the girls.

"Wot's she saying?" the girl cried, thinking the rebuke was directed at her.

He laughed. "Nothing for you to worry about, my dear. I'm the one in trouble."

A few of the girls had decided to work in the munitions plant, as it was closer to home and paid more, but soon regretted their decision. It didn't take long to fill the vacancies they left at the new *Soleil* site, even though it was a considerably longer omnibus ride from the dock area. With Franz still at the old plant, it was taking Sylvie longer to get to work too.

She still took the underground train, but once above ground, because she had always been frugal, took an omnibus rather than a cab. Standing waiting for a bus, often for half an hour, the winter weather left her cold, or worse, soaked.

Walking out after work, she was heading for the bus stop along with several of the girls, when she staggered to one side.

"You all right, miss? You don't look so good."

"Yes, thank you. I'm just cold and wet. My boots didn't dry thoroughly after this morning's journey. I'm so tired of always being wet—what a country this is!"

"Well, it'll be summer soon enough, then we'll all complain about the heat. But you make sure you have a hot toddy when you get home, or you'll catch your death!"

"Thank you, my dear, I'll do that. Ah, here comes the bus at last!"

Sylvie sank onto the wooden bench seat, willing herself not to catch a cold, but knowing the scratchy feeling in her throat was sure to herald one.

Incredibly, within four weeks, once the machines had been bolted to the workbenches and patterns cut ready to sew, *Soleil Soie* was back in production.

It wasn't long before Colette, visiting the factory,

saw that Sylvie was looking very tired. She had also become somewhat short tempered with the girls, which was unlike her. The past few weeks had been exhausting for everyone, and Sylvie was getting on in years.

"Sylvie, let's get out of here and treat ourselves to a good luncheon for a change," said Colette.

"That would be lovely." Sylvie sighed. "I have to admit the noise these girls make all the time is getting on my nerves. If it wasn't for the fact that they are still working while they talk, I couldn't bear it," she confessed.

"Let's go to that smart new hotel, *The Ritz*," Colette suggested.

"Oh my, I don't think I'm dressed for such a fine place, and so expensive," replied Sylvie.

As usual, Sylvie was immaculately dressed, and her objections were overridden quickly.

Colette—as they say—pushed the boat out, and called a hansom cab to take them to the elegant newly built hotel where they could be sure of a wonderful luncheon, despite the shortages.

Shown to a quiet table, Sylvie dropped into a deeply padded, velvet-covered chair, closing her eyes.

"Are you feeling alright, Sylvie?" asked Colette.

"Oh yes, my dear, I'm just savouring the comfort and lovely surroundings. Thank you so much for this treat."

"I have an ulterior motive for asking you out," Colette said.

"I thought you might—what is troubling you," Sylvie replied.

"I am concerned that you are doing too much and that it's making you ill, my friend."

"Nonsense. I am well enough. I just get tired of all the hustle and bustle once in a while."

"We do put a lot on your shoulders, and you take it all without complaint, but I wonder if you should maybe take more time off, say work four days instead of five?"

"And what would I do with all that time? You know the work is my life. I have no family here or back home. You, Franz, and the boys are like family to me, and to be around you is all I ask." She laughed. "When the time comes and I can no longer be an asset to the company—well, then you can fire me!"

"Oh, it will never come to that, but please take time off whenever you need it."

"Thank you, my dear, that's nice to know. Now where is that waiter? I have quite the appetite, and I think a good bottle of wine would be appropriate for this old lady, don't you think?"

They continued their meal happily, each enjoying the delicacies that they had ordered, while wondering how the Ritz came by them, but feeling it was probably better not to know.

CHAPTER 6

Bad News

Neighbors stopped in their tracks at sound of the blood-curdling scream coming from the front door of Twenty-Six Richmond Street in the east end. The deliverer of the news that caused the pandemonium stood waving his arms and rocking from side to side, not knowing what to do with the hysterical woman in front of him.

John Abrams was just fourteen and on his first day as a telegraph boy. He was proud wearing his smart red uniform and hat. Even the bicycle he was to use was red. He was so pleased when chosen from all the other applicants—jobs were still scarce for youngsters needing to support their families. Even now, with so many husbands and fathers conscripted into the swelling, and at the same time, diminishing army, youngsters still found it hard to find work. Gran said the men were needed for cannon fodder. Surely, that couldn't be true. It was 1916 and the papers said they were winning the war after two grueling and bloody years, but few believed their propaganda. Maybe if the Americans got involved, the tide would turn, but so far, Woodrow Wilson kept the United States unwaveringly neutral, apparently.

John was too young to enlist, too young for the mines or munition factories, but to be given a bicycle and just deliver telegrams seemed too good to be true—and it was. Unfortunately, the only telegrams the post office sent these days, told of injuries, imprisonment, or death. John would find that being the deliverer of bad news, the recipient almost blamed him as if it was his fault.

The army had given up sending an officer to tell a family that their son or husband was dead, missing, or injured—just too many of them, and officers were needed at the Front. The job fell to these youngsters who had no idea what the job entailed and how much it would affect them.

Sal O'Ryan, hearing the din from within her own house, rushed out as fast as her old rheumatic legs would allow to the hysterical woman's side. Wrapping her arms around her ushered the weeping woman indoors. She'd had to do it up and down the street far too often, but she was a kind old soul who felt every telegram's contents almost as keenly as the family whose loss it was.

"Blimey, missus, she never even opened it," John said to Sal.

"She don't need to, lad, it's bad news whatever it says," she called over her shoulder to the boy.

Mary Reagan watched along with others coming to their doors to witness this all-too-frequent occurrence. As she felt sympathy for her neighbor, she silently thanked God that her Harold was too old for the army.

It wasn't long ago that she and her mother Maggie had been shopping on Mile End Road, when a rag tag column of young men had marched down the street. Full of bravado, jollying themselves with the thought of excitement and daring deeds, they had taken the King's shilling for enlisting, confident they'd return home heroes. Mary shook her head sadly. How many of them had already returned, maimed, or in coffins? How many would be forever missing, lost in the shell holes and mud of the trenches about which she had read? The newspapers played down the battle horrors, but it didn't take much of a brain to imagine what the boys were going through.

Harold Porter might seem ancient to Mary, but at forty, he was a solid, reliable sort, working at the brewery Although he was older than herself, her mother had kept on insisting that he was a "catch," even if he was almost old enough to be her father. He was a man who kept himself to himself, not spending his wage at the pub on a Friday night, not given to drinking with mates—he didn't seem to have any anyway. He'd courted Mary for six months, their having met at the local market where their hands both grasped the same large turnip, and they had laughed. When he asked her to marry him, her mother said, "There aren't many young men to choose from nowadays, Harold's reliable, and you, Mary love, aren't getting any younger."

Mary was the ripe old age of twenty-four. She'd had offers, but was waiting for the "right" one. Unfortunately, the war intervened and many eligible young men ended up in the services. She wasn't unduly bothered. She was quite content and didn't want to rush into a wartime wedding and either regret it for the rest of her life if he turned out not to be Mr. Right, or worse, mourning the loss should he be the love of her life and not return.

Mary wasn't sure why she had agreed to marry Harold. Oh, he was nice enough, a bit dull though. But her mother Maggie kept on insisting she wouldn't do any better. Not exactly, a love match, but Mary, decked out in her mother's white satin wedding dress, stood at the table in the local registry office, ready to take up married life in Harold's small house, a few streets away from the same house she'd lived in all her life.

Maggie had provided as good a wedding breakfast as funds and available food would allow. Guests, mostly neighbors, provided something from their own meagre provisions, and the mood lightened if only for a few short hours, especially as Harold's employer had provided a fair amount of beer. Strangely, Harold had invited no one, not even a mate from work. He didn't even have a best man, but these days a wedding was more of a necessity than a celebration. Boys going off to war, not knowing if they'd be coming back wanted to experience love if only for a short time. Girls wanted the white dress and to be the centre of attention if only for one day. In wartime, many a girl ended up without her partner for life, but with a baby forever. The lucky ones had their man return, but it was a hollow joy when the man returned dreadfully mutilated physically or mentally. How naive they all were.

The wedding was a good opportunity for women to gather and gossip, looking over, criticizing, or admiring the wedding gifts and the food spread on the dining table. The few men stood in corners, mostly unsmiling, talking in whispers about the current situation in France.

No honeymoon was forthcoming, so the bridal pair just said their goodbyes and headed off to Harold's house. Harold carried Mary's battered suitcase, which held every piece of clothing she had, and she toted a bag of leftovers—nothing should go to waste.

Mary took her suitcase up to the bedroom. She was pleased to find that Harold had purchased new sheets and a rather vibrant green eiderdown. Mum had explained what went on in the bedroom, years ago, but she hadn't sounded very enthusiastic. Maybe it wasn't something to be enjoyed. Mary waited a few minutes but it seemed

Harold wasn't going to follow her up, so she unpacked her clothes, put them away in the wardrobe and drawer space provided. Still waiting for Harold, she returned downstairs and found him standing awkwardly by the fire.

"Why don't we go for a walk? It's a lovely evening," she suggested.

It seemed Harold was more nervous than she was, which seemed odd for a man so much older than herself. Surely, he'd had other women? During their walk, he seemed to relax, and when they returned to the house, things progressed, as they should. If she was disappointed, Mary wasn't going to let on. Harold was a capable lover, tender and gentle, but it wasn't the wild passion that her unmarried friend Molly, had led her to believe lovemaking was. As if she knew!

Harold's rented house was almost identical to the one Mary had just left, but dull and dark, just as a bachelor's house might be expected. Mary scoured Petticoat Lane Market for the odd thing that might make it more homely, while Harold found a few tins of white paint to brighten the walls. Maggie had given the newlyweds a few family photos, but Harold had none and wasn't very forthcoming about his previous family life.

"I can't believe you don't have a single photograph," said Mary.

"Well, they're all dead now, and I guess any pictures got thrown away," he replied.

"Who threw them away then, you?" Mary kept on.

"Mary, give it a rest, will you? Enough to say, I wasn't very happy and prefer to forget," was all Harold would volunteer.

Mary gave up, but it niggled away at her, even though she said nothing.

Life for the newlyweds plodded on. Everything was in short supply. Harold was generous with his wages, but a visit to the shops was a depressing venture. Getting food hadn't been a problem in the early years of the war. Some people panicked at the beginning and stockpiled staples if they had the money.

After a while, they realized that there were few shortages.

However once the newly designed U-boats started sinking merchant ships crossing the Atlantic, it became apparent that much of Britain's needed food supply came from the United States and Canada, and the government began rationing to ensure everybody got a fair share.

By 1916, there was so little wheat available, even for bread, that life suddenly took a severe turn on the home front as prices rose and supplies diminished.

"I can get hold of a couple of chickens and a cockerel," Harold announced suddenly one evening.

"That's lovely, Harold, but I'd only end up having to give the meat away as it would go bad before we could eat it all" Mary replied, somewhat perplexed.

"No my dear, live chickens, for eggs. I could build a

coop in the garden, and we could kill them off for meat, when they stop laying."

Mary was horrified. "Well, I'm not killing them. Will you?"

"I hadn't thought about that. I expect we could take them to the butcher, but let's cross that bridge when we come to it. It would certainly help to have eggs, wouldn't it?" he asked.

"Yes of course, that would be wonderful, but do you know anything about raising chickens? I've never seen a live one, and I don't even know what they eat."

Next evening Harold came home carrying some wooden crates. He set to work making them into a chicken house. It was a ramshackle thing, but when he brought home three hens and a cockerel, they settled in happily that night and seemed to enjoy pecking around the small yard.

Days turned into weeks. If only they would lay eggs!"

"Harold, we're buying corn for these hens and getting no eggs," Mary moaned.

"Give them a bit more time, love. I've been reading up on them, and they have periods where they don't lay. I bet they'll be giving us eggs soon." He kept his fingers crossed.

The damned chickens never did lay, but that Christmas there was plenty of tasty meat on the table!

Vimy, Ypres, foreign names that only signified more

and more loss of life, consumed the newspapers. Now the target was England itself.

"This bloody blackout!" Old Sal was on Maggie's doorstep. "Ain't it bad enough it's dark at five o'clock, without all the gas lights off," she moaned. "There's no coal again," she went on. "I went to Blackie's, then all the way down to the Co-Op depot. Not a lump anywhere. Could you lend us a bit Mags?" she pleaded.

Maggie was short herself and the only option was to keep Sal with her. "Stay here tonight, Sal. It's lonely with our Mary gone, and it seems a pity to light two fires," replied Maggie.

"Don't know, Maggie. I ain't never slept nowhere else since my Donald and me got wed." But the thought of another bitter cold night alone, with Donald long gone, soon changed her mind. "That's kind of you, Maggie. I just got a bit of haddock for me tea. We could share it, eh?"

"Sounds grand, Sal," Maggie replied.

The fish was small, but a number of potatoes fried in lard until crispy made for a satisfying meal. After supper, the two women sat in comfortable silence by the light of the slowly dying fire.

"I'll put a hot bottle in our Mary's bed for you, shall I?" asked Maggie.

"Oh, no dear, I can't manage the stairs at 'ome so I only sleeps in the back kitchen of a night," Sal replied.

"Well that's fine Sal, the armchair is quite comfy,

and the footstool will help. The fire will keep you nice and warm till you doze off," Maggie replied. "I'll just pop upstairs and get you a couple of blankets."

"That'll do just great, Mags, ta love."

The streets were quiet in the blackout. No Zeppelins had come over that night, and the two women soon fell soundly asleep. Sal's house was across the street from the old corset factory that was now the munitions plant. The owner, Mr. Leyh, a foreigner from Belgium had bought the factory just before the war. He was none too pleased to have the government requisition the building and turn it into a munitions factory. The whole street was none too happy either, with all the TNT going into the yard. Still, no one felt very sorry for Mr. Leyh. He was wealthy, foreign, and his family didn't live anywhere near the East End and the dangers of being near the docks or munition dumps.

Once the military took over, he didn't visit the factory. He and his son had set up the corset factory farther away. Most of the girls had gone with him, and it was a real rough lot making the munitions. Didn't do to be soft in there nowadays, you wouldn't last long.

The machines making heavy shells were now running noisily night and day. It was hard on the girls who worked there. Many local girls and women had no option but to work in the hellhole that was the lot of a munitions worker, now that nearly all the men were gone. The wages were good, better than before, but the work was dangerous. A spark could be deadly, but worse was their exposure to the chemicals, acids, and explosives. As time went on, the girls started noticing their skin was taking on a yellow tinge but no one could say why. Even a visit to the doctor, which was most unusual in the East End, offered no diagnosis for symptoms never before seen. Safety was a concern, but often precautions went by the board because of the speed at which they had to work. Accidents happened, but the work had to go on. There was no stopping the war machine.

The Zeppelin that crept over the East End in the dark hours of early morning found its target either by luck or design, and the munitions factory took a direct hit. The resulting explosion was the like of which had never been heard before. Every fire engine available raced to the scene, but the fire was so fearsome, the only real option was to let the building burn to the ground. Only a few of the girls got out, some horribly burned. Neighbors, jolted out of bed, rushed out into the street and were shuttling buckets of water to the scene of carnage, but they soon realized that anyone who was coming out was already out, and the death toll was mounting. Houses either side of the road, and as far as the eye could see, were on fire or destroyed, Sal's included.

People sleeping in those houses never had a chance. All neighbors could do was help the wounded and watch the destruction. Through the morning, they went door to door, crunching over glass littered pavements, checking on friends and even strangers. Many houses suffered major damage and were as uninhabitable as those completely destroyed.

Maggie and Old Sal were jolted from sleep as the explosion shook the house to its foundations. Maggie raced downstairs, the fire from the factory lighting the room, even though it was streets away. "Jesus, Mary, and Joseph," Sal cried, suddenly awakened in the half-light. "What happened?"

"It's the munitions factory, Sal, it's exploded! Oh, my God, the girls in there," Maggie cried.

"Maggie, me 'ouse, is it still standing?" Sal cried. "I know I should be thinking about the girls, but I'll have nowhere to live if it's gone."

"Stay here, Sal, I'll go and see. They'll need all the help they can get, but it's too much for you. You stay and make tea. There's a thermos in the larder. I'll be back as soon as I can."

Maggie knew that tea wasn't going to solve anything, but she needed to keep Sal occupied and away from what was going to be a devastating scene.

The Germans were throwing everything they could at London. Bombs fell from the zeppelins, those great bloated air balloons, like giant slugs. The British artillery guns were not very effective against them, and the airships didn't need any guidance on a moonlit night. They just followed the glistening Thames all the way to the center of London and its docks.

Bad enough London being pummelled, but ships all round Britain were targets for U-boats as well. If the war didn't end soon, Britain would be starved into submission as the merchant navy continued to take heavy losses. Even small fishing boats weren't safe from the floating mines.

That morning, as the sun came up, the street was eerily quiet. Maggie's daughter went round to her mother's house, hoping it hadn't been damaged as it was a fair distance from the factory. Harold's house was far enough away not to be damaged other than a couple of broken windows, but she knew her mother would be frantic until she came round to reassure her. The three women sat at the kitchen table, too shocked to say much. "I've got to get to me 'ouse" Sal cried. "But I don't reckon there's much left."

"Was it an accident, Mum?

"No, they're saying it was a zeppelin. Bloody bastards! I've never seen anything like it. Those poor girls inside didn't stand a chance."

Mary was shocked. She'd never heard her mother swear before, but she herself echoed her mother's thoughts.

The three of them made their way to the factory, or what was left of it. Maggie had to support Sal as they surveyed the destruction. Her house was completely gone, just a jagged pile of smouldering bricks, as were most on either side and across the street. Sal and her neighbors hugged each other, some crying, some angry, others just silent.

"Who's dead then?" Sal asked bluntly.

"The Wilson's, all of them and their lodger. Edwards, Barkers, Simpsons. Just about everyone, 'cept you, Sal. How come you came through without a scratch then?" asked a neighbor.

"I was at Maggie's 'cause I 'adn't got any coal and she put me up," Sal said.

"Well, for once it was lucky we have a coal shortage!" said her neighbor, tartly.

"It's not right. I'm old. I shouldn't be the only one left. It's not right," Sal moaned, tears beginning to run down her cheeks.

"Will you take 'er in, Maggie," whispered the same neighbor. "She 'asn't anyone as far as I know. We'll all be taking someone in if they've nowhere else to go. Don't know when or if these places will get fixed, It'll be hard to find materials, let alone builders!"

The East Enders, were a rough and ready lot, but when the chips were down they pulled together, willing to help each other.

"Of course, come on, Sal, we'll sort summat out," replied Maggie.

"Me things, what about me things?" Sal moaned.

"Don't you worry, Sal," said Maggie, knowing there was nothing left of Sal's things, but Sal was lost in her thoughts and didn't reply. They made their way slowly down the destroyed street. There wasn't anything left to say.

Sal never really recovered from the events of that night. The carnage and loss of her home and neighbors, took the fight right out of her and the old feisty woman became a mere shell of her old self.

CHAPTER 7

Zeppelin

The night the zeppelin that destroyed the munitions factory crept over the East End, Franz and the family were safe in their beds, all except Robert who was out on the town. Before he got his orders, as he knew he would all too soon, he was living recklessly, cramming as much into his days and nights as he could, thinking he probably wouldn't see his next birthday. He could have volunteered and been guaranteed an officer's rank, but he had no illusions that he was officer material. He didn't want to be 'other ranks' either, and prayed the war would end before he got conscripted. He'd do his bit, eventually, but he was no hero. Maybe he should declare himself a pacifist, but he really wasn't. He thought himself a coward, but was it cowardly not to want to die. Surely, he wasn't the only one, but he couldn't bring that sort of shame to his parents, his father in particular. He considered Ernest the lucky one. A bout with rheumatic fever when he was a toddler in Spa, left him with a dicky heart which would certainly exclude him from active service.

Frequenting the gambling clubs, bars, and pubs of the West End, Robert often arrived home in the early hours of the next morning, much the worse for drink. This particular night, Robert was frequenting one of the rougher areas of East London, along with a few pals that had so far escaped the draft too. Staggering into the Spotted Dog, dingy with years of pipe smoke clinging to the ceiling and walls, Robert was first at the bar. "Four pints of your finest ale, my good man," he drawled.

A group of hefty Dockers in their usual spot after work looked up from their benches beside the glowing embers of the fireplace, and one started to rise to his feet. The barman, despite his girth, quickly rounded the bar to set himself between the two groups. In the war, they might all be on the same side, but the classes never mixed socially. These upper crust "Charlies" were certainly unwelcome in the East End, and the locals were ready to put them in their place.

"Now, lads, I don't want any trouble. This isn't your local, and you've had more than enough tonight. On your way now."

In their befuddled state, Robert and his cronies were taken aback.

"Wha'd' you mean? We're not causing trouble," slurred one of them.

The barman, anxious to keep a lid on the situation, used his bulk to edge them to the door. "It's closing time, off you go boys."

Robert and his friends, finally taking the hint that trouble was brewing, turned and left, laughing loudly. Inside, the local lads, itching for a fight, were up on their feet, ready to follow. Drunken tempers were rising, as was the noise level.

"Who do they think they are? Toffs coming to our pub, laughing at us. Come on, lads, let's give 'em what for!"

The barman, still blocking the door, knew these lads would make mincemeat of the strangers, and not wanting to witness any violence—after all wasn't there enough going on in France?— tried to defuse the situation.

"Lads, you've time for one more pint—on the house, eh, and how about a tater pasty?

"Yeah," the cheer went up. "Pints all round barkeep, you're a good man!"

Thrown out of the Spotted Dog pub and ignorant of how close they had come to a beating, Robert and friends were making their drunken way on foot along the Mile End Road, when to the south the sky lit up as if it were midday.

"Jesus! What the hell was that?"

Suddenly sobered, Robert cried out, "My dad's munition factory is over that way. God, it must have gone
up! Come on, we'd better see if we can help."

Running all the way, they arrived as wounded were
stumbling out of the burning buildings and locals were
organizing buckets of water in a futile attempt to put out
the flames. The raging fire made it impossible to get into
the factory and find the girls working there. Only a few of
them came stumbling out in panic, pleading with the by-
standers to find their workmates.

Robert and his friends were soon covered in soot,
their hands blistering as they plied the buckets hand over
hand into the inferno, or tossing water over the fortunate
survivors whose clothing was smouldering or actually
burning.

"I've got to get to my father and tell him what's happened," Robert told the police officer who seemed to be
in charge. "He owns the factory, he should be told at
once."

"Right, sir, we'll go in my police motor," the officer
replied. "There's little more I can do here. Let me just
inform my sergeant to take charge of the men, and we'll
get going."

Racing through the quiet streets in the early hours,
they were soon in the West End. Arriving at the house,
Robert jumped out of the car and ran up the steps to
pound on the door, quite forgetting he had a key.

Franz, suddenly awakened by the din outside, ran downstairs and flung open the door. "What the hell? Robert, what have you done now?" he shouted at the blackened spectacle in front of him.

The police officer, somewhat slower on his feet lumbered up the steps. "Now, sir, the lad's done nothing but distinguish himself," he said. "I'm afraid your factory, the one making munitions, has exploded, and your son's been helping the wounded and trying to put out the fire."

"God in Heaven, how many dead?" Franz whispered.

"No one knows right now, sir, but I think you should come with me," replied the officer.

"Of course, but I must telephone the ministry first. I'll be with you in a minute. Robert, are you hurt?"

"Not at all, Pa, but it's terrible, all the houses around are gone as well. I think the death toll will be huge," Robert said shakily.

Once the ministry had been informed, Franz hurriedly dressed, explained briefly to Colette what had happened, and left her before she could ask any questions.

"I'll come with you, Pa," Robert said, but Franz said he was to stay and comfort his mother, who would surely be in a state by now.

Ernest joined Franz, having heard the commotion, and they both left with the police officer, making their way through the silent streets, arriving at the factory as dawn broke and the scene fully exposed the devastation.

Several men in army uniforms met them at the site.

Franz jumped out of the car, and ran to them. "Dear God, I told you this would happen—how many dead?" he gasped.

"We don't have a final count, sir. There are a number of wounded as well. There's nothing you can do, sir, I suggest you return home. The site isn't safe but we will keep you informed," said one of the military officers.

The gruesome task of bringing the bodies out of the still-smoldering ruins was the job of the fire brigade, some of whom were just elderly volunteers. Other folk helping the police were now concentrating on the adjacent plots, that were once homes, and trying to control the gathering relatives searching for their loved ones.

Occasionally there was a shout of joy, but mostly it was silence punctured by crying as they found their family members.

A group of men too old to fight stood to one side, talking and occasionally looking toward where Franz and Ernest stood. One of them called out to no one in particular, "There 'e is, the German—'e done it, got the Bosch right to our doorsteps."

"Now, now, Stan, no call for that," said a police officer standing nearby.

Well known to the police, Stan was often in trouble for his hotheaded temper.

"Well, he's got a German name 'asn't he? Maybe 'e's a spy!"

"Stan, I won't tell you again, pipe down," said the officer, anxiously looking round for reinforcements should the situation get out of hand.

Franz could stay silent no longer. "Sir, I am a Belgian Jew, not a German. I left Belgium because I was afraid for my family's safety with all the anti-Semitism that was arising there. Why would I be making shells in my factory, for the British, if I was a German spy?"

"Well, I was just sayin," Stan said, somewhat contritely.

"Right, you've said quite enough, and if you can't be any help here, I suggest you go home, Stan. The rest of you as well," the constable called out, raising his voice, but he was relieved that the situation had calmed down. He turned back to Franz and Ernest. "Come along, sirs, nothing to be done here, I think you should go home as well."

They made their way back to the police vehicle and the two men drove home in silence, both too shocked to say anything.

As they arrived at the house, Ernest turned to his father. "Why did you tell those men you were Jewish, Pa? Are we Jewish? If so, why did Robert and I go to an Anglican Church School"?

Franz sighed. "We are, but for our safety here, it seemed wise for your mother and me to keep it to ourselves. Even in England, especially in the East End, there is quite a lot of anti-Semitism, and I just wanted us to live in peace. Religion has never played a big role in my life, but it's better to be considered a Jew than Bosch! However, now that you know and are adults, you and Robert must choose your own path. I will not stand in your way if you wish to take up the faith."

This was a lot to take in, and Ernest was amazed that his father would admit to being Jewish, having hidden it for so long, but he was right. Things could have got very ugly if he hadn't spoken up.

Once at home, Franz walked straight past Colette and Robert into his study, shutting the door. Colette wanted to comfort him, but she knew he had to deal with this in his own way. Robert, now he was away from the fire, began to feel the burns on his hands. Colette turned to see him beginning to go into shock, almost falling into Ernest's arms.

"My God," she cried. "Look at his hands, Ernest. Get him into the dining room, and I'll fetch Mrs. Scott, she'll know what to do."

Mrs. Scott was the cook and, though not a nurse, had dealt with the minor kitchen mishaps in the past.

The staff, beginning to arrive for their day's work, were surprised to see the family up in various states of dress and in such a state. Those that lived in the East End quickly filled the others in with the details of what had happened overnight.

Mrs. Scott came upstairs with a small tin that sufficed as a first aid kit but, upon seeing, Robert's hands declared, "He must go to the hospital at once. This is far more than I can deal with." She wrapped each hand in clean tea towels and helped him drink the tot of brandy that Ernest had poured for all, servants included. "Hail a cab, will you?" she asked Maisie, the housemaid, who was loitering by the stairs.

When the hansom cab arrived, Colette and Ernest helped Robert down the front steps. "Mrs. Scott, would you tell Mr. Leyh where we have gone? And perhaps he would benefit from a glass of brandy too."

Standing at the study window, Franz had already downed several brandies as he watched the rest of the family disappear into the foggy morning.

St. Jude's Hospital was busy with the injured from the explosion. With the local East End hospitals working at capacity, St. Jude's was taking in wounded as well. Colette gave Robert's name and injury and was told to wait, warned that it could be a long one. After what seemed like an eternity of watching the horribly burned and wounded, Robert was finally seen. His burns, though serious, would heal in time, and as long as he kept them clean to prevent infection, he should feel no ill effects, other than some scarring. Through his pain, it finally dawned on Robert that this was what England was fighting for. No longer would he sit back. He'd volunteer just as soon as his hands healed.

Once the military took command of the ruined factory, there was nothing more for Franz to do, but it didn't stop him brooding and feeling guilty that this should have happened, even though it was in no way his fault.

Surely, the munitions plant wouldn't be rebuilt on the same site, in deference to the locals who had suffered so from the tragedy. Residents wondered if they would get their homes rebuilt, as there was little compensation and even less building materials. It was a black time for the East End.

CHAPTER 8

Harold's death

It all seemed so futile to spend days cleaning house, cooking whatever could be found in the shops, when all this suffering was going on across the Channel and now at home. The only good news on the street, just eleven months after the explosion, on Christmas Eve, Mary gave birth to a girl. The baby had dark hair, bright blue eyes, and a happy disposition. Baby Joannie brought great joy and lifted the spirits of the house and its inhabitants. Even Sal, lost in her thoughts most days, began to brighten a little, happy to hold the baby and croon old songs to her.

Mary's mother was to come to dinner on Sunday, and, as Joannie was to celebrate her first birthday that week, Harold went out on Saturday to buy a bottle of stout to celebrate. He was never out long, unless he was at work.

After two hours had passed and he hadn't returned home, Mary began to feel uneasy. When a knock at the door came, she ran to the door. 'Did you forget your key?"

However, on opening the door, she saw Gladys, a friend who also worked at the brewery, standing there.

Mary's smile faded and a feeling of dread came over her heart. "What has happened," she cried, knowing that this was not a social call.

"Can I come in, Mary?" Mary opened the door wider, and Gladys stood just inside. "I'm sorry to bring bad news, Mary, but Harold has met with an accident."

"Oh my God, where is he—at the hospital, St Anthony's?" Mary cried.

"Um, no, I'm sorry he's at the morgue—he died near the brewery when a dray horse bolted and ran 'im down. The police came and took down all the details from the office manager. I told 'im you and me was friends, and I'd come and tell yer. Is there anything I can do? Do you want me to stay?" Gladys asked.

Mary's felt the blood drain from her face, but no tears came, the shock was too sudden. "No, no—thank you, I'll go to my mother's," she said in a monotone.

"Well, I'm very sorry, Mary—I'll be going then," replied Gladys, relieved that Mary wasn't going to get hys-

terical as so often happened when bad news had been delivered.

Mary shut the door behind her and leaned against the
cool wood. Her heart was pounding, she couldn't breathe,
and she just wanted to drop to the floor and have it swal-
low her up. Instead, trance-like, she got her coat and hat,
put Joannie in her perambulator, and started for her
mother's house. Neighbors passing by, having no idea
what had happened, were confused when their greetings
met with a stony stare. They'd seen that look often, but
on the faces of soldier's widows. What could be wrong
with her? Her man wasn't at the Front. Mary didn't stop
to explain.

Maggie opened her front door and looked at Mary,
whose tears were beginning to roll down her cheeks.

"Mum, he's dead, what will I do?" she blurted out.
"How will I manage?"

Maggie plopped down in the nearest chair. "Unbelievable—how could he be so stupid!" she retorted when
she heard what had happened.

"Mum, that's an awful thing to say—he didn't do it
on purpose!" cried Mary.

They sat together, tea going cold on the table, each
wrapped up in their own thoughts. Old Sal, still living
there, away in her own world, didn't seem to take the
news in.

Maggie, ever practical, came to her senses first.
"Well, what you have to do is register his death so you

get a widder's pension. First off, we'll have to go to the 'ospital, get a death certificate, and find out what 'appened. We'll get Sal to watch young Joannie, and then we can get the bus to St. Anthony's." Maggie turned to Sal. "Sal, you got to watch Joannie for us. We'll be back soon. Take her for a walk in the pram, but wrap her up warm."

"Yes, walk the baby," replied Sal in a monotone.

No morgue was inviting. This one was no exception, just a bleak little building with barred windows, behind St. Anthony's hospital. The two women gave Harold's name to a severe-looking woman behind a glass partition and were told to wait. After what seemed an eternity, a small man in thick spectacles and a white coat came out to speak to them.

"I'm sorry I can't give you the death certificate, it's already been picked up, and Mr. Porter's remains have been taken away," he said pompously.

Maggie was the first to take this in. "What do you mean, we can't have the death certificate? My daughter's his wife! And where have you taken him?" she blustered.

The man in the white coat turned red in the face and stuttered "I—I'm sorry, his wife—"

"His wife? I'm his wife," whispered Mary.

"I'm sorry" he began again. "The woman who came had the marriage certificate, dated 1902."

Maggie turned to Mary. "Oh my Gawd—he was one of them what you call its—a bigamist—he was married before! Did you know that Mary?" she cried.

"Of course not, Mum—he never said," Mary whispered, tears again welling in her eyes.

"Humph," Maggie said. "And it looks like he never got a divorce! I must say this pretty kettle of fish. We'll have to look into this or you're not going to get any widder's relief. And I thought he was such a good catch. Just goes to show. Well, at least we won't have to bury 'im!" she said harshly.

"Muuum—what will I do?" More tears were falling down Mary's face and she was beginning to get hysterical.

The morgue clerk was still hovering, not knowing what to do or say.

"What's this 'wife's' name and address then?" Maggie demanded, gearing up for a fight.

"I don't think I—er—can give you that information, madam," he retorted.

Maggie drew herself up to her full five foot two. "I don't give a toss what you can and can't do—I have to take this up with the authorities, and I *need* to know! *Now*!" she bellowed.

The man caved in. This sort of thing had never happened before, and he wasn't used to such unpleasantness. It was obvious the woman wasn't going to leave without what she wanted, and he wanted for her out of his office as soon as possible.

Scribbling down the name and address, he handed over the piece of paper.

The explosion had shocked Maggie and Mary to the core—now Harold's death! It was hard to take in. Getting Old Sal settled, and gathering up bits and pieces of clothing and furniture for the survivors, they'd no time to seek out Harold's previous wife.

Now, a few weeks after, Maggie broached the subject with Mary. "I think we should go and see the woman, don't you, Mary?" she asked.

"What's the point, Mum? She's legally his wife and I have no claim," replied Mary.

"We don't know that for sure. He might have got a divorce—I think we should go, if only for Joannie's sake," Maggie argued.

Mary had found work in a local green grocer's shop and didn't want to lose a day's wages on a fool's errand, but to appease Maggie she agreed with a sigh. "She lives south of the river, Mum. That's a long journey and the fares will be a lot."

"Don't you worry about that, we'll go on a Sunday, so you won't lose money, and I've got a bit put by for the fares," Maggie reassured her.

The following Sunday morning, they deposited Joannie with Old Sal, and the two women set off. Buses were rare on Sundays, and it took several hours for them to get to Battersea where Ivy Porter lived.

"Oh, Mum, I don't know if I can face her," Mary cried as they reached the front gate of Ivy's home.

"We haven't come this far, to back out now, my girl,"

retorted Maggie, who marched up the path and rang the bell.

A middle-aged woman peered round the door, opened just far enough to see who was there.

"Are you Ivy Porter?" Maggie began.

"Oh, it's you. I was wondering if you'd be calling. You're that bastard husband of mine's floozy," she called over Maggie's shoulder to Mary, who was standing behind her.

"Watch yer tongue. My daughter's no floozy. She married him all legal and that, or so we thought," Maggie snapped.

"What do you want from me then?" Ivy replied a little more contritely.

"My daughter has a baby by 'im, and no money or anything. Did you divorce him?"

"No, I didn't. He just went off one night, went out for a drink so he said, and never came back. Sorry I'm sure about the kiddie, but what do you expect me to do about it?" Ivy replied coldly.

"Well, I would hope you'd give the child something from the estate, at least," Maggie retorted.

"Nothing to give. I own this house. He never had any money, other than his wage. Now, if you'll excuse me—"

"Just a minute. If you haven't seen him for years, how did you find out he was dead?" asked Maggie.

"Must have been the records at the brewery. Police came round and told me," Ivy replied tartly.

"You mean he never even changed his work records. Oh, Mum, how could he? He didn't care about me or Joannie at all."

"Never mind that now, girl. We'll be going then. Thank you for your time, *Mrs.* Porter."

"He was a complete waste of space, useless, no ambition. I was glad to see the back of 'im. Good riddance!" she shouted after them.

Maggie was bitterly disappointed that there was nothing for the baby, but Mary hadn't expected anything else. They were both quiet on the way back, both locked in their own thoughts.

"Guess that's it then. You'll have a hard time of it, my girl, but you know you and Joannie will always have an 'ome with me and old Sal. You know that, don't you."

"I know, Mum, but what a dreadful woman. She must have been a horrible wife. Poor Harold. I could forgive him for walking out on her, but why, why didn't he divorce her? He wasn't a waste, he was good and hard working. I think he did love Joannie and me."

"We'll never know now, will we, dear?"

CHAPTER 9

Racketeering

Even though these were difficult times, Franz still expected Colette to be the homemaker and mother she'd always been, but Colette had other ideas. Women of her class had rarely worked before. Life had not prepared her to do anything useful outside the home, and, bored with the few household duties she oversaw, she began to think about what she could do to help the war effort, other than knit scarves with friends at their gossipy tea afternoons.

No longer needed on a day-to-day basis, now the clothing factory was up and running, Colette was still eager to help the war effort. It was yet another cold, wet autumn day, and Colette was agitated and restless.

Franz was poring over the household accounts. "Whatever is wrong, Colette, you're pacing up and down like a caged animal," asked Franz innocently.

"You cannot be so churlish as to expect me to sit here doing nothing, when everyone else is working to end this God awful war," she cried.

Franz was taken aback at her vehemence, and he really didn't need any more aggravation in his life. "Do you want to work on the buses or should I find you a position in munitions?" he replied somewhat sarcastically.

"Don't be ridiculous, and don't patronize me," she retorted sharply.

"I'm sorry, dear, I'm just tired like everyone else, *and* I have to pay higher wages to the house staff just to keep them. Sometimes I think they are holding us all to ransom!" he moaned. "The munition girls are earning three to four pounds a week already and can you believe I had a deputation of six women waiting for me outside *Soleil* this morning, demanding a raise in pay? How they knew I'd be in today, I don't know. I'm sure Robert wouldn't have mentioned it, but I'm glad I was or he would have had to deal with them alone, and I dread to think what concessions he would have given into!"

"Oh, Franz, making munitions is such awful work and so dangerous. You cannot begrudge them a decent wage."

"I don't, but the ministry pays them, and I can't match their rate at *Soleil*. It got quite ugly, and I was afraid I'd have to send Ernest for the police. I tell you, Colette, this war is dragging the country down so far, I doubt we'll get through it, let alone win!"

It was just the beginning. Even with their higher pay, workers in other munitions plants actually went on strike. Shortages were cutting deep into the psyche of most British families. It was only a matter of time before Britain went the way of Russia and anarchy broke out.

Franz bent over the table, his head in his hands, "I don't want to worry you but the news is bad. So many men are dying. Everyone's had enough. I just don't know where it will end."

Colette was sorry. She hadn't realized quite what a strain he was under. Rising, she went to him, putting her arms around his shoulders. "I'm sorry, I shouldn't have made such a fuss."

Franz, always protective of Colette, had tried to shield her from the worst of the news, but she was stronger than he knew and she was determined.

"I need to do something, Franz. I feel so useless."

"Look into something that will make you feel useful, my dear, but you know I do appreciate all you have done for me, and running this house is quite demanding of you."

Later that week, she read an advertisement in the morning paper that women were needed by the Voluntary Aid Detachment to help the medical staff of Guy's hospital. Now this was worthwhile work, she thought, and carefully cut the advertisement from the page.

Once Franz had left for the day, Colette took a cab to Guy's Hospital. She hadn't realized it was south of the river, and if she was taken on, she would have to rely on an omnibus, as a cab there and back would be far too expensive.

Arriving at Guy's and explaining why she was there, she was shown into an ante-room and told to wait. A few other women joined her; mostly well-spoken women, who were also hoping to help the war effort.

A woman in a nurse's uniform came in and introduced herself as Matron. She looked across at the well-dressed, pampered women and began to speak. Before she had finished two women had excused themselves, and the rest sat open mouthed after hearing what they would see and do, should they have the stomach to stay. Colette stayed.

It was an eye-opening experience for her. The doctors were treated like gods and the nurses ran around obeying every command barked at them. If doctors were gods, Matron was the devil. Every nurse was mortally afraid of her, and her rounds of the wards incurred frantic cleaning, tidying of patients, their beds and cupboards. When she arrived, uniforms had to be immaculate, even if the nurse had just finished cleaning up vomit, excrement or dressing a putrid limb. Colette was kept out of everyone's way in the sluice room where doctors didn't visit, and Matron delegated its inspection to the ward staff nurse. Colette cleaned bedpans. How she hated the work. Thank heavens it was only two days a week. She was the lowest of the low. Even the student nurses treated her with veiled contempt. Every day, she swore she would quit, but the thought of telling Franz she couldn't cope with the work kept her going. She had her pride, after all, and she had said everyone had to do his or her bit for the war effort. Once she had proved herself, the ward sister had promised she'd be given different tasks. Anything would be better than bedpans, Colette thought.

Franz wasn't happy! He was rarely happy these days. He worried incessantly about money, or lack thereof, and Colette being away from the house for hours on end wasn't helping.

"Franz, we all have to help in any way that we can," Colette said for the umpteenth time.

The war machine ground on. Conscription was taking men in ever-increasing numbers, with thousands never to return. The hardship of daily living kept on worsening for those left behind.

Dinner, such as it was, was late again as household staff left for better paying jobs elsewhere. To the family's relief their cook, Mrs. Scott stayed on, and a daily now came in to help Maisie the housemaid with the cleaning. It was better than having no help. That night, Colette broached the subject of money.

"Franz, I was speaking to Mrs. Baxter this morning at luncheon, and she said that they were making a fortune from the government contracts. Why aren't we?"

"Colette, in order to make a fortune from government contracts, one has to supply cheap, substandard goods and charge the government full price. I could not, in all conscience, do such a thing," he replied.

Colette was mortified. "Are the Baxter's doing that—I cannot believe it!" she cried.

"I have no proof, but if Baxter is, he's not the only one. Many people are making money on the bodies of our soldiers. It is disgusting," he replied vehemently.

A few days later on her way home from the hospital, Colette rushed into the house, letting the door slam loudly behind her. Breathlessly she ran into Franz's study. "Franz, you will never guess what I just saw. I was coming home on the tram and, as we passed the Baxter's, the most extraordinary thing—Mr. Baxter was being escorted down their front steps by two military policemen and he was in handcuffs!"

"How bizarre," Franz said with a smile beginning at the corner of his mouth.

"Do you think it has something to do with the black market?"

"I wouldn't be at all surprised," was all he would say.

CHAPTER 10

Daniel

As Britain declared war on Germany, so too did the rest of the colonies, and Australian soldiers deployed all along the Western Front along with Canadians and South Africans. Daniel Simpson, an Aussie, was one of thousands conscripted or volunteered, into a war that really had nothing to do with them. Australia was part of the Empire and, therefore, the call went out to all allies. Boys eager for adventure, knowing they'd probably never have the opportunity again to see the rest of the world, ended up on the alien shores of Europe. Daniel, a fit young man, strong and able, had given up on schooling at fourteen to strike out for the opal fields of Northern Australia to make his fortune. He was used to harsh conditions—extreme heat, deadly snakes, scorpions, but his experiences on the Front in the mud and filth would give him nightmares for the rest of his life.

In 1917, he and many of his compatriots launched an attack south of the town of Ypres, in Belgium. Although the attack was successful, nearly seven thousand men became casualties of war and those that could be, were sent to England for medical attention that was not available behind the lines.

Daniel considered himself one of the lucky ones. He had a severe leg wound, but the medic at the base camp thought his leg might be saved, if he could get to England for surgery. After an agonizing wait of several days for transport, he was loaded into a horse drawn military ambulance with several others in far worse condition, to endure a hair-raising and dangerous ride to the coast of northern France. Once there, using crutches he limped slowly up the gangway onto a transporter to cross the English Channel where he'd undergo surgery and, hopefully, recover.

Landing on the Dover coast, he and the many other Australians with serious wounds were loaded onto stretchers at the port, to await yet another journey. The Salvation Army was there to offer hot tea, clean clothing, and a chance to wash of the grime and lice if they were able, in makeshift bathrooms.

A matronly woman in civilian clothes passed along the stretchers, stopping at each one. Her accent betrayed she was upper class, but she spoke kindly to each, despite the chaotic scene and the horrifying sights she saw.

"Good morning, young man," she said to Daniel. "Can you tell me your name, identity number, and unit, please?"

When Daniel replied that he was from Australia, she smiled. "It might be a while before we can get you back there, but we will do our best. Now, are you injured, other than your leg?"

To those unable to fend for themselves, due to their injuries, especially those blinded by gas attacks, she spoke so gently; consoling and comforting, putting her hands into filthy uniform pockets to extract any information she could. Once she had written an identity ticket with all the information she could ascertain, and pinned it on their jackets, they were bundled into ambulances and driven away to the various local hospitals. Daniel learned later that the woman was a relative of the royal family.

Daniel, however, was driven to Dover's central station, put on a train for London with the more seriously wounded, where, they were told, the best surgeons would attempt to repair the horrendous, often gangrenous wounds that endangered their lives. As he lay on his stretcher, Daniel tried to steel himself against the rocking and bumping of the train on the rails. Every bump sent a knife like pain through his thigh. He kept telling himself he was lucky, especially when he looked over at one of his wounded companions. The poor boy, for that's all he was, was delirious with pain and thrashing about, only causing his wounds to bleed more. Daniel doubted he'd come through surgery.

Arriving late that same day at Guy's Hospital in Southwark, Daniel thought he'd been sent to a lunatic asylum as the building was big, dark, and forbidding in the gathering gloom. Once inside, nurses, doctors, and civilian aid workers rushed here and there, and soon he found himself bathed, shaved, his wound temporarily dressed and, joy of joys, a clean pair of pyjamas. Moved to a long ward with a dozen beds, a smiling woman with a foreign accent set bowl of mushy slop in front of him. H ate ravenously—it was better than anything he'd had in days.

"I'm sorry the food is not very good," she said, turning to go.

"Please stay, I was wondering where I am. Am I in London? You don't sound English."

"Yes, for sure you are in London, and you are right, I am not English, I'm Belgian. I'm not usually on the wards, but I think I have had a promotion as I'm usually on bedpans." She laughed. "My name is Mrs. Leyh, but you can call me Colette, if you want."

"Thank you, Colette, believe me this soup is wonderful," he said sleepily.

"You sleep now, perhaps I will see you tomorrow, although I may be demoted again," she said, laughing again.

Daniel drifted off—the last thing he heard was her tinkling laugh. Next morning, after a most peaceful sleep, despite the pain in his leg, the occasional sirens, and small explosions, which he assumed must be near the docks, they wheeled him into surgery where an ether mask soon sent him into oblivion. Waking up was quite another thing! Pain wracked his leg from hip to ankle but a nurse came quickly upon hearing his yells, carrying a hypodermic needle and blessed relief.

"Do I still have my leg, nurse?" he begged.

"Of course, you do, Dr. Brown did a wonderful job, and you will be up and about in no time," she said comfortingly.

Dr. Brown did do a good job and, compared to others, Daniel was extremely lucky, but out of bed in no time—no way! Rehabilitation and learning to walk on a leg that was now two inches shorter than it was would be a challenge. Still he was alive, and a limp wasn't going to stop him. Might keep him away from the Front, though—he sincerely hoped for that.

Weeks later, he was transferred to the Salvation Army rest home, where there was plenty more freedom, and the lads could venture into Central London to see the sights if they were able. Wouldn't hurt if they could find some girls too. It had been a long time since they had had any female company.

Maggie was worried about Mary. She went to work, came home, took care of Joannie, but she no longer laughed and rarely smiled. Still, to be fair, there was little to smile about. Old Sal had passed away that winter and both women missed her. She had just had a cold, but it turned rapidly into pneumonia, and she passed away quietly, never having fully recovered from the explosion and loss of all her possessions.

"Mary," said Maggie, looking up from her newspaper one evening after their frugal meal. "There's a tea-dance at the Variety next week. Why don't you and your friend Elsie go and have some fun. Make a nice change for you."

"No money for daft things like that, Ma. You know it takes everything I earn to keep us," she retorted.

"Oh, girlie, I can find the sixpence for you to get in. You really should get out and meet some fellas. There's lots of soldiers in town, but make sure yer careful, a lot of 'em are foreigners!"

"I don't want a fella, Ma, but it would be nice to forget the war and dance for a while," Mary replied wistfully. "All right, I'll ask Elsie. I'm sure she'll want to go."

That Saturday, after work, Mary rushed home, got out the tin bath, filled it with hot sudsy water, and luxuriated in it, in front of the kitchen fire. It took a lot of effort to fill the tin bath. Umpteen kettles had to be set to boil on the Aga, and they were heavy to lift and carry, but it was worth it. Wrapped in a towel, she hung her hair over her face to dry by the heat of the fire. She brought her best dress out of the mothballed wardrobe and aired it.

Trying the dress on, Mary was horrified to see that it was now several sizes too big.

She called down to Maggie. "Ma, what am I going to do? My dress hangs on me like a sack. I can't wear it like this. Bugger it, I won't go!"

"Now, now, don't be so hasty, let's see what we can do," consoled Maggie, although she wasn't sure what could be done in short order.

"I'm going round to Emily's. Give me the dress. If anyone can do something with it, she can." Maggie's friend Emily was a seamstress, but this would be a challenge even for her.

Rushing round the corner to Emily's house, she pounded on the door.

"God almighty, Maggie, whatever's wrong."

"Em, I need this dress taken in, and I've only got half an hour! I finally persuaded my Mary to go to a dance, but she's lost so much weight, her dress just hangs on her," she explained.

"Don't panic, come in, and let's have a look," Emily replied calmly.

Emily's old sewing machine was always set up, and once she had re-threaded the spool with the right color thread, she quickly ran a new seam on either side.

"Now, this isn't what I'd normally do, but I think it will be all right. I've got a pretty belt that will hold it in nicely as well. Just let me get it, and we'll both go and see if it works."

Back at the house, Mary was sitting by the fire,
thinking that the dress was a lost cause, but if anyone
could make this work, Em could. The front door banged
as Maggie, closely followed by Em, returned.

"Let's see if this will do," said Emily.

Mary shrugged the dress over her head. It looked a
lot better than it did before.

"Thank you so much, Em, I didn't think anything
could be done so fast. It looks great!"

"I think this might just do the trick," said Emily as
she put the belt round Mary's waist. Made of filigree of
silver, the belt was obviously an antique.

"Ooh, Emily, it's beautiful, but it must be worth a
fortune. I can't possibly wear it. Suppose I lost it or it got
damaged?"

"I hardly think you'll do either, but it does have a
safety pin just to be sure."

"My, I haven't seen you look that pretty in a long
time, luv," cooed Maggie. "You have a great time and
don't worry about Joannie, I'll see to her. But do be careful and stick with your girlfriend," she cautioned. "And
don't drink too much and miss the last bus," she added.

"Oh, Ma, I'll be home by ten, I assure you."

She picked up Elsie from her house in the next street,
and the two girls made their way to the bus stop, chatting
excitedly about how the evening might unfold. Elsie was
as, they say, 'done up to the nines' with her hair curled,
wearing her best dress and her mother's old fur cape

.She'd even rouged her cheeks and colored her lips, something—Mary thought, but didn't say—made her look a bit cheap.

The Variety was a dance hall in Central London, so it took the girls a while to get there. Neither liked the Underground. It was gloomy, smelled dank, and the heels on their shoes had a habit of catching in the wooden escalator steps, risking a fall. It was preferable to stay above ground, but the two buses the journey needed took a lot longer.

The lights of the Variety were subdued outside, but inside it was reminiscent of life before the war—colored lanterns, a four-piece band, little tables set around the dance floor, and the only difference, a number of soldiers propping up the bar, checking out the girls as they entered. After they had paid for their tickets, the two of them pushed through the double doors to the dance hall, stopping short as they took in the room.

"Jeez, Mary, I feel a hundred years old. Look at all those girls, they can't be over twenty, any of them," moaned Mary's friend. "We don't stand a chance."

Elsie was anxious to meet a chap, having lost her fiancé at the very start of the war. Some girls never took up with another fellow once they'd lost theirs, but Elsie was a romantic and didn't relish a lifetime alone. The two girls took their place at a table, and ordered lemonade from the barmaid.

Mary became aware of a young man's eyes on her.

She felt embarrassed, at first, but eventually their eyes met, and she smiled at him. Seeing the two girls come in, the young soldier had taken a liking to Mary at once, but how could he ask her to dance? He'd only just learned to walk again and it didn't look as if he'd ever be able to dance, not that he could even before his injury. Not much chance of dancing in the opal fields.

When the music stopped, he took his chance and limped over to her table.

"Miss, my name is Daniel. I'm not able to dance, but I'd like to buy you ladies a drink and talk, that is, if it's all right with you."

"You are welcome to sit, but there's no need to buy us drinks, we already have one, thank you," Mary replied primly.

Seeing that he was looking at Mary as he spoke, Elsie, not wanting to play gooseberry, made an excuse to leave the two of them and twirled away into the surprised arms of a handsome officer who was passing by the table.

Daniel seemed happy to just sit and watch. He wasn't much of a conversationalist, but Mary, finding out he was an Aussie, took the lead coaxing him into talking about his home in Australia and how he looked forward to going back. Despite the improving flow of talk, Daniel seemed to drift away at times. Mary assumed he was thinking about home, but in reality he was already beginning to have flash backs to the Front, and was having difficulty remaining in the present. Trying hard to keep the conversation light and not frighten Mary off, he didn't mention the nightmares, or the sudden bouts of anger which had him punching the walls, or crying like a baby.

It seemed they had only just arrived, but the time had flown by, and it was already past nine o'clock. Mary made her goodbyes to Daniel, while looking for Elsie on the dance floor.

"I'm going to be in England for a while, I think. May I call on you?"

"Oh, Daniel, I live in the East End, and your rest home is south of the river. It'd be quite a journey for you with your bad leg."

"Just give me your address, and I'll see if I can find it. The leg—well, it's got to get better, and the more I use it, the sooner it'll be strong again," he countered.

Finally locating Elsie, Mary almost had to drag her off the dance floor to catch the bus home. She'd given Daniel her address, never expecting him to call on her, but it had been a pleasant evening, and she didn't regret the time she had spent with him, even though she hadn't danced once.

Daniel found his way the first time, only getting lost once, and he enjoyed seeing London from the top of the bus. As Mary had said, it was quite a distance, but the route took him past several famous sites that he'd only heard of, or read about in books. London was like nothing he'd ever seen before. It seemed to go on forever. Adelaide, his hometown was a big city, by Australian standards, but London—*hell, it must go on miles!* Before he left England, he'd make sure he visited the museums and art galleries. Maybe Mary would like to go with him, he mused.

"This is your stop, mate!" called the bus conductor.

Coming out of his reverie, Daniel was confused as he took in his surroundings. "I'm going to Waltham Street, can you tell me which way?"

"Go down Walsingham Road till you get to Findley Street—that way," said the conductor, pointing. "You only got to ask, anyone'll tell you."

"Thanks, mate—first time in these parts."

"Thought so—you're an Oz aren't you—your lot took a hammering outside Vimy, didn't they? Well, good luck to you, lad."

Daniel struck off in the direction of Findley Street, thinking he might have misheard the directions, as it seemed an awful long way. It was probably just that his leg was weak and beginning to ache.

All the streets looked much the same, row upon row of gray terraced houses, but eventually he found Waltham Street, having asked a couple of boys playing marbles in the gutter. He was more than surprised when Mary opened the door holding a toddler in her arms.

"Daniel! What a surprise! Come in, come in. You must be exhausted. There are so few buses on Sundays, however long did it take you to get here?"

Daniel had to admit he was relieved to sit down, but

pleased with himself that he had found his way through the maze of streets. Over tea, Mary explained briefly about Joannie and how she'd thought she had been married before.

"Crikey, that takes the biscuit—what a bastard—your husband, that is, not the kiddie!" Daniel added quickly.

"Well, that's over and done with. Now I just have Joannie to think about, and Mum too, of course."

Daniel became as regular a visitor to the East End as he could manage. As time went on, if things developed as he hoped, Mary's child might prove a problem.

Finally, the war to end all wars ended. The relief and celebrations were huge. Even the king and queen came to the East End.

Maggie scowled sourly, despite her jubilation. "They could have come before and seen what the East Enders were going through, instead of hiding out in Buck House, far away from the bombs. After all, their rotten relatives started it!"

Mary took Joannie to watch the royal couple and their entourage pass down Mile End Road. Joannie, still too young to understand, waved her little flag and watched in amazement at the parade. Later, she enjoyed the street party even more, where the residents had made every effort to provide sandwiches and jelly for the children, who were, by and large, running amok among the dining room tables and chairs that had been dragged out into the street for all to sit. Eventually they took the chil-

dren indoors as things became too boisterous when the
men and women, drinking as much beer as they could,
became louder, if not rolling drunk.

Daniel had joined Maggie, Mary, and Joannie, and
much as he would have liked to drink away the awful
memories, he was becoming attached to Mary and didn't
want to spoil his chances by appearing a drunkard.

Some months later, Daniel was de-mobbed and had
his passage back to Australia, surprisingly on a passenger
liner, not a military ship. It was chaos getting soldiers
who'd ended up in England back to their homes around
the world. So many ships had sunk, records were incom-
plete or lost, so it wasn't all together surprising that passenger ships were pressed into service once again, having
been de-commissioned from war service. If shipping records were sketchy, it made sense, with so many dead and
missing, that the soldiers' records were unreliable too.
Some men simply disappeared into the folds of the English landscape, finding lodging and work, sorting out the
paperwork later if they needed to.

Daniel was determined to go back to the Australian
opal mines where he had been making good money. He
had savings in the Royal Australia Bank, and, as soon as
he had enough, he'd get out of mining, head south and
find work in a less harsh environment. He desperately
wanted Mary to marry him and leave for Australia with
him. Would she come with him without the kid? There
was no way the child could live in the outback. The opal

mines in Woola Bella were no place for children. They were no place for women really, but he was terrified that if he left Mary behind, he'd never see her again.

CHAPTER 11

Ernest's bombshell

Colette was happy. Her boys, now grown men, had escaped the war, and were working for their father. Franz's factories were ready for restoration to civilian status.

The bicycle factory was fine. It just needed the machinery brought back once the sewing machines were gone. How to go forward at Soleil Soie was more of a problem. Should they continue making work wear, or return to making lingerie? Times were changing fast, and it would take some thought. Then of course, there was the ruined munitions site. What to do with that?

Eventually, Franz decided to return *Soleil Soie* to its original format and dispense with work wear. The bicycle factory would continue as it had before the war. The munitions site would stay a hole in the ground until a buyer was found.

At home, the house was running with reduced staff as few wanted to stay in service when better jobs were available in this new bustling economy. However, the daily along with the parlor maid and Mrs. Scott, were coping fairly well.

Franz, still rueing his decision not get into motorcar manufacturing, had given in to pressure from the boys and purchased a car from Robinson's which he drove proudly to and from the factories.

Robert was still wayward, new women in his life every few months, and was spending rashly. It seemed the war had not matured him, and his father no longer had any control over him, not that he'd had much in the past.

Ernest, dear, steady Ernest, was overseeing the accounts for both factories now in the process of restoration to their previous states. Colette wondered if he'd ever marry. He didn't seem to have much interest in women. Robert teased him mercilessly, but even that didn't seem to bother him. Recently, Ernest seemed even quieter and it was a shock when he gave his news at dinner.

"Mother, Father, I have to tell you something. I hope you will hear me out, and not be too angry," he began.

Colette and Franz looked at each other, then at him then at Robert, expecting that Ernest was going to divulge some mess that Robert had gotten himself into, again.

"I have to tell you all that Maisie and I were married today," Ernest stated bluntly.

"Maisie? Who the hell is Maisie?" Franz demanded of his wife.

Colette stared at her son in shock. "Maisie is the housemaid we engaged last spring," she whispered.

Franz exploded. "What do you mean you married the house-maid? Why for God's sake?"

"Maisie is expecting my baby, and I did the honorable thing," Ernest explained.

"You don't fuck the help, and you certainly don't marry them, you fool." Franz was not to be mollified. "I can't believe this," he raged.

Colette blanched at the use of the foul language Franz was shouting for all to hear, both upstairs and down.

"Well, well, well, old goody two shoes, gets the help in the club." Robert laughed. "Good for you old boy—didn't think you had it in you."

Franz was almost apoplectic. After years of dealing with Robert's antics, he reacted irrationally to Ernest's news.

"You will leave this house immediately, and take your floozy with you. Don't bother coming to work—you're finished. I don't want to see either of you again."

"Franz, No! Please don't do this. Whatever the circumstances, the child will be our grandchild," Colette cried.

"Be quiet, Colette. Nothing will change my mind. I will not have such shame brought into this house."

It was nothing more than Ernest expected. His father was old fashioned as far as morals were concerned. Sorely tried by Robert's escapades, this to Franz was the final straw.

Ernest gathered a few clothes and his bankbook, with its small amount of savings, into a bag and went in search of Maisie.

He found her crying in the kitchen. She as well as Mrs. Scott had heard the ruckus coming from the dining room.

"Come on, Maisie, get your things. We have to go," he said coldly.

"Where are we going to go, Ernest? I don't have any family."

"Lot of good families are—seems like we're on our own. Get a move on, will you?" he replied stonily.

Ernest wasn't sure how his life had come to this. He was the good, reliable son. He had always felt he had to prove himself to his father, to prove he was a man, despite his frail appearance. Why did he have to have had rheumatic fever when he was a child? It had kept him out of the army. Wouldn't it have been better to die a hero, than see the looks of scorn on the faces of people who didn't know he'd been rejected? He'd received more than one white feather during the war, which cut him to the core.

Handsome, reckless, Robert, who'd done his best to stay out of the fighting. had tried to join up after the explosion, but he'd been rejected as his hands hadn't healed well enough for him to fire a weapon.

Ernest had had little success with women, but for some reason he'd been attracted to Maisie.

Maisie, quiet little Maisie, always on hand, always sympathetic, had listened to him without criticism and encouraged him, not physically at first, but he felt a rapport with her, and it had led to surreptitious outings and eventually to a sexual relationship.

He didn't love her. He wished he did, but when she'd tearfully told him she was pregnant, he felt obliged to do the right thing. After all, he wasn't a cad.

The sudden silence in the Hanover Square house was deafening. Franz retreated to his study, closely followed by Colette, who wasn't going to let the matter rest.

"How could you do that?" she cried. "You would banish your son, in this day and age? Wake up Franz—this is a new century. You need Ernest, more than he needs you probably!"

"I do not want to discuss it, Colette. He has brought shame and dishonor to our family," he replied coldly.

"Well, you may have banned him, but I certainly have not." I shall have contact with him, his wife, and their child, you can be sure of that!"

She turned and marched downstairs to the kitchen, desperate to see Ernest before he left and she lost him for good. She found them saying goodbye to Mrs. Scott and pulled Ernest aside.

"Ernest, I cannot undo what your father has said, and I wish I could help you both, if only financially, but as you know, I have no funds of my own."

"It's all right, Mama, we will be fine," Ernest said with more conviction that he actually felt.

"Please send me your address when you are settled, Ernest. I don't want to lose you," she sobbed.

"I will, Mama, don't worry." Turning to Maisie, he picked up her suitcase. "I'll let you know where to send my things, Mama, if you would be so kind as to pack them up for me."

Robert, suddenly realizing the seriousness of the situation, had followed his mother a few minutes later. "Look, old chap, I'm sorry for what I said. I know you're in a bit of a jam, but really, I'm proud of you for doing the right thing. If you need anything to get you started, just send word to me. Truth is, I'm lucky not to be in the same boat, the things I've got up to over the years, and you've always been there for me. Take care, old boy. Good luck to you both."

As the door closed behind them, Colette collapsed weeping, onto a chair at the kitchen table.

Mrs. Scott, the cook, who had heard every word from the scullery, came in, a cup of tea in her hands. "There, there, don't you fret, madam. All families go through this sort of argy bargy. It'll be all right, but I think you should drink this."

Colette took a large gulp of tea through her tears, nearly choking on the liberal dose of cooking brandy in it.

The remaining Leyh family began picking up the pieces of their lives following the war and Ernest's departure. Returning the factories to their previous occupations was a tedious and frustrating time. Finally, both factories were back in business. Madame Mireille, ancient as she was, still held the reins at the corset factory and was taking production into the latest range of intimate apparel, which no longer included the heavily boned corsets, but more seductive under-slips, and the newest thing from France—brassieres. This name didn't seem to translate, so they just kept the French word for it, along with negligees, which sounded so much more exotic than nightdress and housecoat. Obviously, men would not be happy about making intimate apparel, so the factory remained in the capable hands of the local women. With the men coming back, ready to resume the jobs they had left to go to the Front, the women who had kept vital services and factories running were loath to give up their independence.

Before the war, the suffrage movement had been gaining momentum and, to appease women and suppress their increasing militancy, the government was forced to give the vote to women over the age of thirty. It was a start, After all, hadn't they done 'men's' work all these years?

Even with the return of the men, women now out-numbered them. Marriage was not always an option, and they were often unwilling or unable to give up working. It was certainly a time of complete change in society. Not only did women continue to work outside the home, but their manner, decorum, and dress became a way to ex-press their newfound freedom.

Sylvie came for one of her regular lunch dates with Colette. After greeting her, Sylvie could see that Colette was still angry with Franz about Ernest, and now, no longer needed at the hospital, she was bored with the job of just running the house.

"Colette, I have been thinking," Sylvie began. "As you know, I came out of retirement to help the family business here in London, but I am getting tired, and I need to slow down. The factory is doing well, but I see new opportunities that I am just too old to pursue, or ap-proach Franz with."

"Oh, Sylvie, we have relied far too much on you. Certainly you must take it easier, or even retire, though how we will manage without you I just don't know," ex-claimed Colette.

"Well, before I go out to pasture, I would like to see the women's work wear production continued not dis-pensed with, and the lingerie department expanded. I was disappointed that Franz decided to stop work wear production. I see women in the work force more and more in the future. They will continue to need our clothing and they will have money of their own to spend on prettier things. The time is right to expand."

"Sylvie, you are so right, but Franz is keen to get the bicycle factory making motor bikes. I don't know if he will be able to finance expansion in *Soleil Soie*."

"Well, that is for Franz to work out. He would have two capable sons if he wasn't so stubborn, and I'm sure he will find investors if he can't finance it himself."

"If you retire Sylvie, who will run the intimate apparel factory?"

"There are several bright young women that I have been training in management, and there is one person who is more than capable, but currently doesn't work for me," Sylvie replied.

"Are you suggesting we recruit someone from another business, Sylvie? That doesn't sound like you."

"No, no, the obvious choice is you, my dear. You have hidden your talents for way too long."

Colette was shocked "Oh my, I know nothing about business, Sylvie."

"Not right now, but with my coaching, and your designing, you would eventually be a great role model for young women and an asset to the company. You don't have to do it all, there are others to take care of the financial side, and, as I said, I have several girls ready to take on purchasing, distribution, and the like."

"This is all so sudden, I must think about it," replied Colette, but already plans were whirling in her head.

"Well, we will approach Franz together if you like, and the sooner the better," said Sylvie.

Franz's interests were now directed toward motorbike production, and though he would never confess it, he was not as fit as he used to be. When Sylvie suggested that Colette might take over *Soleil*, his initial reaction was to refuse, but on further thought, it made sense. A man just didn't have the softness to design these new intimates. It was different when it was just corsets. They were more of an engineering project. Yes, he must allow Colette to take the reins.

Colette began working in earnest. Sylvie, true to her word, had found several women to move into management, and they were working well. Colette was designing alongside Sylvie, learning from her years of experience. There was so much to learn apart from design. It was hard to find the delicate fabrics and what was available was expensive. Bargaining was Sylvie's second nature, but it came hard to Colette.

"Right now, we are short of French silk and Belgian lace. We will make short runs of quality garments, but to keep up our production we must make lesser quality garments," Sylvie explained.

Colette gasped. "But we've never made substandard clothing, Sylvie."

"And we never shall, but until the economy picks up,

we must make our lines in keeping. Silk from China, and machine made lace will suffice for the time being. Women still need underclothes, but only the very few will buy our premier lines for the next few years."

"I have so much to learn, Sylvie, and I want to prove myself to Franz. Will I ever get to grips with everything?"

"In time, my dear, in time. I'm still here to guide you, don't worry."

The munitions factory was still derelict, following the explosion, and it worried Franz that it was such an eyesore, and a reminder of the horror the East End had experienced.

He needed to think hard about where the old bicycle factory was going to go in the future. How often he regretted not staying with George Robinson, who was now manufacturing cars for the masses at prices many could afford.

Bicycles were always needed, and Franz still couldn't entertain the expenses of getting into motor cars, but motorbikes? Now, that was something else. It would probably make more sense to refit the old bicycle factory than re-build on the old derelict munitions site.

Diligent as always, Franz started making enquiries about motorbike production. Up until now, they were pretty much only used by the military, but he thought these would be cheaper transportation that the lower classes could afford.

Franz was still much of a snob, in that he didn't mix socially with "other ranks" as he called the general populace, but he knew they were the key to his future.

Even through the worst of times during the war, Franz had maintained his credit worthiness and, being on good terms with his bank manager, arranged a loan at a favorable rate to begin retooling for the manufacture of motorbikes.

Franz hired any able man that applied at the factory site to get it retooled quickly. Despite the difficulty of getting materials and equipment, the men worked hard. It was good to be building instead of destroying, as they had been for the past four years. When the factory finally reopened, those same men were offered jobs on the line. Returning servicemen too disabled for heavy line work, were found clerical positions where possible, until the plant was fully *manned*, literally. The tide seemed to be turning backward for women, and some who had so diligently worked during the war, found themselves none too happily back in the kitchen, dependent on men to hand over their wages, and not earning for themselves. Wherever possible, Franz would find a position for a war widow, or the wife of a severely disabled ex-soldier. Snob he may be, but he had a profound sense of duty. What a pity that sense did not extend to his son Ernest.

CHAPTER 12

Maisie & Ernest

Ernest could never afford a house in London. Even renting would be difficult with the housing shortage. Maybe they could find something a distance away, and being away from Franz might be a good idea. He decided that it might be pleasant to live by the sea and the closest and easiest to get to by train was the town of Southend-on-Sea at the mouth of the River Thames. He'd been taken there once, before the war and had fond memories of the town.

"How do you feel about living by the sea, Maisie?" he asked while they were eating the meagre breakfast provided by the proprietor of the modest bed and breakfast accommodation they had stayed in overnight.

"The sea's a long way from here, isn't it, Ernest?"

"Well, not the real sea, but Southend, at the mouth of the Thames might be nice."

Maisie acquiesced. She'd never been in a position to argue about anything, so if Ernest said they'd move to the moon, who was she to say differently?

Southend had been a haven for London day-trippers, keen to get away from the smog and soot, if only for a day. The seafront was bustling in summer months with trippers enjoying the amusement arcades and bracing walks on the long pier that reached out into the mouth of the Thames River—over a mile, they said. Ernest remembered it was fun to watch the steamers arriving at the end of the pier with laughing East Enders debarking, eager to spend their money on fish and chip dinners, kiss-me-quick novelty hats, and other such nonsense. Children had played on the beach, building sand castles, waiting for the tide to return and wash them away. Mothers and fathers rented deck chairs with brightly striped seats, or sat on blankets, while eating ice-cream cones. Not too many braved the cold water to swim, but a paddle with trousers rolled up or skirts hiked was enough for most.

The town was quick to bring its image of fun and foolishness back, and war weary Londoners were once again boarding the train for a day out.

Yes, Ernest thought, this was where they would make their new start.

Maisie was an East Ender, but losing her parents at

the age of ten, she'd only known the anonymity of living in an orphanage until she was old enough to find work. She was one of the lucky ones when she found herself placed in Dr. Barnardo's, an orphans' village in Barking-side. There were hundreds of girls housed there, but she learned the art of domestic service, which would eventually be her lot in life.

As a teenager, she had to leave the safety of the orphanage when staff there found her employment with the Leyh family. She was relieved to find herself working for a good family and, as the only housemaid, she worked hard but felt appreciated by the mistress. The cook was kind enough and, thankfully, there was no butler to boss her around either. Overall, it wasn't a bad place to be. She counted her blessings because it could have been a whole lot worse. There were two grown sons in the family, and Mrs. Scott, the cook had told her, in no uncertain terms, that they were off limits and to "know her place." She also warned her that Robert could not be trusted, and a pretty face was fair game to him, so be careful!

Ernest, the older son was always kind to her, and silly, romantic fool that she had been, she let things go further than they ought. At first, it was just talking, then he accompanied her when she went shopping for things Mrs. Scott needed. Eventually, the inevitable happened under the cover of darkness in the park across from the house. Ernest when he came to his senses was mortified and kept apologising. Maisie took it in stride, thinking nothing could happen the first time. The relationship such it was, stopped as quickly as it had started until Maisie told Ernest tearfully she was pregnant. Never in her wildest dreams did she think he would marry her when she told him. Those upstairs, never married downstairs. It was usually an automatic dismissal from the house, without a reference, and "make sure never to darken our doorstep again!"

Dear, solemn Ernest had done right by her, but at what price.

Later that morning, they arrived on foot at Fenchurch Street Station, to catch the train to Southend. Once inside the huge terminus, Maisie clung to Ernest's arm, fearing she might lose him in the hustle and bustle of the morning rush. Detaching himself from Maisie's grip, Ernest directed her to sit with the luggage beneath the towering four-sided clock and wait while he purchased tickets. He was soon back with two second class tickets. His budget suggested he should have bought third class, but he just couldn't bring himself to do so. Passing through the gate at the platform, after showing their tickets to the guard, they located their carriage, and it wasn't long before the train whistle blew and the mighty engine began jerking its heavy load forward. Soon it was chugging easily, and Maisie watched the squalid rear gardens of London's East End finally disappear and give way to gently rolling fields. She'd never been on a train before and loved the clackety clack of the rails, the smutty steam when she put

her head out the window, and when the sea came into
view she was enthralled. The tide was out, and she could
barely see the ribbon of water in the far distance. Brightly
colored fishing boats listed aimlessly on the mud flats. As
the train pulled in to the station at Leigh-on-Sea, she
could see the fishermen waiting for the tide, busying
themselves mending nets, drinking, and talking noisily at
the Peter Boat Pub. Steam rose in great clouds from the
cockle sheds nearby and the aroma of the cockles boiling
in great vats assaulted the nose as they waited for the
train to move on.

Once they arrived at the quaint Southend Central Station, they asked directions to the nearest estate agents to
find a suitable place to rent. Even bed and breakfast living would quickly eat into Ernest's savings so it had to be
soon. When they had a place to live, he'd look into finding work. He'd had the presence of mind to secure good
written references from several of *Soleil Soie's* suppliers,
believing that, as it had turned out, he would no longer be
employed by his father.

Footsore from walking from one available rental
house to another, Ernest decided the best one was a three-
story just off the High Street. It was clean enough, but
dowdy, had a small back yard, but the front door opened
straight onto the pavement. Best of all, the rent was af-
fordable—for the time being anyway, but Ernest would
have to find work soon.

A house was more than Maisie could ever have expected or hoped for—her own home. It didn't matter how small, or that it wasn't in the best area—to her, it was a palace. She was determined to make her marriage work, be the best wife, and Ernest would surely grow to love her.

The house was empty and they could move in immediately. Fortunately, the previous owner had left a few sticks of furniture, a kitchen table and two chairs, a bed frame, but no mattress, even two "tall boys" that, with a good scrub, would suffice. As they took possession of their new home, a neighbor was busily cleaning her front step. It didn't need cleaning, but she was curious about who was moving in. Ernest had gone inside, but Maisie stopped to say hello to the woman who introduced herself as Mrs. Tomlinson. From her, Maisie was able to ascertain the layout of the town, the best place to buy groceries, and she offered to take Maisie to the second hand market, where she could find decent furnishings.

With the few pounds, Ernest had given her, Maisie and Mrs. Tomlinson scoured the second hand shops for the basics, leaving Ernest to look for work. One second-hand shop had most of the items Maisie needed and, as it was Wednesday, and most stores shut at one p.m., the shopkeeper agreed to deliver everything she had purchased from him, later that afternoon. With any luck, she'd have everything in place by the time Ernest returned home.

The movers dumped the various pieces of furniture

on the doorstep, hardly delivered! Ethel, Mrs. Tomlinson, watching from her front window, came out to help and, between the two women, they carried everything indoors. It was a struggle to get the felt ticking mattress upstairs but, laughing, they managed and flopped it onto the existing bed frame.

Two days later, after pounding the streets looking for work, Ernest came home in good spirits, having been offered a junior position in the local bank, following confirmation by his referees.

He started work at the bank soon after, but found it tedious and far below his abilities. But a job was a job, and he would have to wait until something better presented itself.

Maisie was in seventh heaven and proud of her home, now that she had scrubbed it from top to bottom.

To make ends meet, she suggested they advertise for a lodger, just temporarily of course, she assured Ernest. He wasn't keen, but agreed reluctantly, and the next day Maisie put a card in the newsagents window, advertising a room for rent to a "clean living, non-smoking gentleman." Hastily Maisie called on Ethel Tomlinson to help her find another bed. Once again, a visit to the second hand stores provided the necessary furnishings.

Walter Edge answered the advertisement, having been seconded to the local water board, and needing temporary lodging. He was quiet, and assured the couple he was, as the advertisement had required. His references were sound and he was soon occupying the topmost bed-room.

Ernest was used to things being just so and was more like his father than he cared to admit. Everything had to be right, and he began to treat his wife like the servant she had been before.

Maisie ran the house like the clockwork he demand-ed. Every evening, she served dinner promptly at six p.m. The table linen had to be immaculate with full comple-ment of cutlery on the table, even if there was only an entree and dessert. He was satisfied with the Royal Doul-ton dishes, and only Maisie knew that there were several pieces missing in the set for eight.

Early next spring, Maisie doubled up in pain as the first pangs of her labor began. She was thankful it was a Saturday and Ernest was home, so that he could get to a telephone to call the midwife. Maisie hadn't had much pre-natal care, but she was healthy and had no problems. On one of her few visits to the doctor, she had met Nurse Boosey, the local midwife, and she was happy when she arrived, took charge, and shooed Ernest downstairs to boil kettles of water and instructions to keep out of her way.

Frederick Robert was born early the next morning, healthy and bawling. When allowed in the bedroom, Ern-est briefly kissed his wife, stroked the baby's head, and said he had to get back to the kitchen.

"We are running a guest house, Maisie. Someone has

to see to our guest," he explained, somewhat sourly.

"I've asked Ethel, next door, to cook the evening meal for the next few days Ernest. Perhaps you could manage the breakfasts?"

Ernest was not happy to have his routine interrupted, but with Maisie in bed for at least a week, there was nothing else to do. Possibly, he could ask Mrs. Tomlinson to do the shopping and breakfasts, although he was not one to ask for help. When he had gone, Maisie burst into tears. She had so hoped the baby would warm Ernest to both of them. Ethel, sensing all was not as it should be between Ernest and Maisie, dropped by to see if they needed any help and to visit Maisie and the baby. Ernest was grateful he hadn't had to ask for help, saying he had some things to get from the chemist for Maisie and would appreciate it if Ethel could pick them up for him. Having assured him she would, she went upstairs to see Maisie who was no longer crying, but puffy eyed and obviously upset.

"Now, now, all new mothers get the blues, and all new fathers are totally useless, so dry your eyes, have a good sleep, and let me see this baby." She peered into the crib. "Oh, my, Maisie, what a beautiful boy and such dark hair. I'm just next door if you need me," she offered. "You only have to bang on the wall," she said, knowing that Maisie had no family of her own and Ernest would be back to work the following day. "Ernest has asked me to pick up a few things for you from the chemist. Is there anything else you need while I'm out?"

"I'll be fine, and thank you so much for all your help, you are such a good friend," murmured Maisie, who was almost asleep.

Exactly one week later, Maisie was back on her feet. Ethel, as good as her word, had kept things going in her absence, and she was always eager to see the new baby and help. A succession of lodgers occupied the spare bedroom as Dolly, Jack, Emma, Arthur, and Theresa followed Frederick's birth in regular succession every two years, until the little house was overcrowded and funds remained extremely tight. Maisie was happy with her brood, the house was often noisy and in the state of chaos that only children could cause.

Ernest became surlier in his demeanor as he resented Maisie for ruining his life. Often overlooked for promotion, which annoyed him intensely, he mostly ignored Maisie unless he had a complaint to lay upon her. Maisie tolerated him—he was her husband, after all—but her focus was her children and all her energy went to providing them with a loving home.

Monday was washday, rain or shine, and it was up to the children to help bring the dirty clothes and bedding down to the scullery before school.

"Dolly, get them out of bed will you," was the rallying cry. There was always a rush to the bathroom and, more often than not, the youngest found herself hopping from one foot to the other as she waited for her turn in the lavvy.

Despite Ernest's dour demeanor, the children were boisterous and made as much fun as they could out of the household chores.

"Will you get a move on, you lot? I've got to get the sheets downstairs," cried Dolly.

There was always a lot of shouting and confusion as the six children tried to get ready each morning.

"Jack, give us a lend of your socks, will ya?"

"I can't find my shoes, Ma!"

"Who's taken my school shirt?"

As long as they all had something on, it didn't matter who was the actual owner. In various stages of dress, they tumbled down the stairs to the kitchen, where a huge pot of porridge was steaming on top of the range. Having fed everyone, Maisie took advantage of a few quiet moments once everyone left. She was exhausted by Saturday, trying to manage the house, lodger, and family, so she shooed the children out of the house early to get up to whatever it was that children got up to when left to their own devices. They spent all their free time on the seafront, which extended from the Shoebury Garrison in the east to the cockle sheds at Old Leigh. They would roam up and down as far as their legs could carry them. A favorite place was the pier, which was rumoured to be over a mile long, extending into the deep water of the estuary.

Across from the pier and up a side street wafted a

sweet, sickly smell that drew the children like magnets. It was the Southend Rock Company where they made the pink peppermint sticks of rock candy.

"They're making rock. Come on, let's see if we can get some."

The children peered through a grimy window to watch the ribbon of pink goo slide in one end of the conveyer belt and come out the other in sausage like rolls. Even more intriguing was the fact that inside the "sausage" it said *Southend-on-Sea* all the way through it.

"Lemme see, lemme see," cried Theresa, the only one too short to see through the window.

"Give her a boost, Jack," Emma said. "If you don't, she'll only start grizzling."

Hoisted up between two of them, Theresa pressed her nose against the window to get a look.

"Oi you, kids, I've told you 'afore, if she falls, I'll be for it!" It was the elderly caretaker. If he was in a good mood, he'd bring out a bag of broken bits for them, but mostly he was crabby and told them to 'bugger off." But there was always a chance…

The seafront was always busy in summer, with London day-trippers, but for two weeks in August, it was crazy, with more people than ever coming to see the thousands of electric lights strung across the road from the pier to the Kursall Amusement Park about a mile away. The aroma of fish and chips, beer, and candyfloss wafted out of the various kiosks and numerous pubs, each one vying for the Londoner's hard-earned money. This was the favorite time for the children.

Unknown to Ernest, who would have put a stop to it immediately, the older children would make the youngest, Theresa, stand under the pier on the beach and sing for pennies.

"Aw, go on Trees, give it a go," urged one or other of the boys. "If you don't, we'll leave you here," they threatened, knowing they wouldn't dare.

For all she was little, Theresa had a loud, if not always tuneful voice, and she could belt out any popular tune that was on her mind. Because Theresa was not only small, but also cute, on the verge of tears, the day-trippers often drunk, were generous with their money.

Later, the children would take the money and squabble with each other about who was to view the *What the Butler Saw* stereoscope or buy a great glob of candyfloss, which they would all share. A good round of singing would enable the children to indulge in both a giggle on the pier and the candyfloss, arriving home hot and sticky.

School was an obligation that all the children, except Frederick, found to be an intrusion on childhood fun. The younger ones were often in trouble, but Frederick worked hard and always had a good report card until the day he came home for lunch with bloody knuckles.

"How'd you do that, Freddie?" Maisie asked as she took care of the wounds.

"It was Mr. Jowett. He hit me with a metal ruler."

Maisie bristled "Whatever did you do? Whatever it was, he should never have hit you like that."

"I was talking, showing Brian how to work out a math problem," Freddie answered.

"Well, we'll see about that." She put on her hat and coat and marched out, leaving the children wide eyed at the table and Frederick trying to wrap his knuckles with a bandage.

"Don't make a fuss, Ma," Frederick called after her.

Maisie was short in stature, but nobody hurt her children. She barged into Freddie's classroom and demanded what right the teacher had to inflict such damage on her boy.

"You had no right," she yelled, looking up to his face, several feet above hers. "My Freddie's hands will be his fortune—you know how good he is at the technical drawing. If you've ruined his chances you'll, you'll—"

"Mrs. Leyh, I will reprimand the children as I see fit," he said, sitting down with a weary sigh.

"No, you won't. Not if I have anything to say about it." And with that, Maisie hauled back and gave him a tremendous right hook to the nose. "See how *you* like it, you great bully!"

"Aagh. I'll have the law on you for that," Jowett mumbled, as he tried to staunch the flow of blood from his nose.

"Oh, will ya? And me being all of five foot one, and you a hulking great six foot odd. Who do you think they'll believe when I tell them you came at me?"

With that, she turned and marched out.

Maisie never talked about her family, having lost them when she was so young, but during the few times her father had been around, he had taught her the tricks of his trade—bare knuckle boxing!

All of Masie's children moved immediately to another school.

Of all the children, Frederick was the brightest. Clever and artistic, he excelled at school, hoping to go to university. However, it was the mid-1920s and the economy was faltering. When the crash came in 1929, Ernest sadly told Frederick he would have to leave school and find work. No university for him.

CHAPTER 13

Mary & Daniel to Australia

With his passage booked, Daniel now had to persuade Mary to come with him.

"Mary, I want you to come with me to Australia," he began. "Until I can get enough money together, I have to go back to the mines up north, and it wouldn't be good for Joannie, but if your mam would agree to keep her for a year, we could send for them both and then we could live in Sydney or Adelaide," he rattled off.

"Daniel, how can you ask me to leave Joannie?"

"It's the only way to make this work. I wouldn't ask you otherwise," he countered.

"Couldn't I stay with your mother if it's not a suitable place, this Woola Bella?" Mary asked.

"Not sure about that, I haven't been in touch with her since I left to come to England," he replied.

"You mean she doesn't know you've been injured, or even alive? How could you not tell her Daniel? She must be worried sick."

"Well, we didn't get on, and she sort of washed her hands of me when I left school and went opal mining."

"Oh, dear, this isn't going to be a good start to our life together if your mother doesn't even know I exist." Mary was torn. She had become very fond of Daniel, despite his moods, and wanted a new start—but leaving Joannie... "Let me see what my ma says. It will depend on her and, to be honest, I don't think she will agree."

Surprisingly, Maggie was in favor of what Daniel suggested. "It's only one year. You know Joannie will be safe with me, and you won't get a better offer. Think of it, sun all year, a new country not bogged down by tradition and all its class snobbery. What more could you want?"

Daniel had no ring to give Mary, but he had one prized possession that he offered to her.

"Mary," he said, pulling a small leather pouch from his waistcoat pocket. "This is the only thing of value I have, and I want you to have it. It's my lucky opal—it's a good one, you won't find better." He dropped the stone onto the tablecloth where it glittered in the light of the coal fire. "It's what they call a black opal," he added.

"It's a most unusual thing," Mary said, turning it this way and that to catch the light. "It's beautiful, but it's your lucky piece, I can't take it away from you, can I?"

"Kept me safe...well, safish through the war, and I know it should be on your finger, 'cause you keep me safe now. We can take it up West and get it set—I want it set in gold, nothing but the best for my Mary," he went on.

"Oh, Daniel, it's beautiful, and I will wear it, but there's no need to spend what a jeweler in the West End will charge." "We'll take it to Uncle Solly on the Mile End Road. He'll see us right," she suggested.

"A Jewish jeweler? Are you sure," Daniel asked uncertainly. He like so many had an inbred distrust of the Jews.

Mary bristled. "Uncle Solly has been my friend since I was a little girl. I went to school with his son Micah. I would trust him with my life," she said angrily.

"All right, all right, I didn't mean anything," Daniel said hastily, before he upset her even more. "We'll go see Uncle Solly tomorrow, okay?"

It wasn't far to Sol's shop on the Mile End Road. He was one of many Jewish shopkeepers along there where the stores held a wonderful assortment of merchandise. It was good to see the East End come alive again, trucks delivering, people coming and going, with much shouting and good-natured bantering going on.

Daniel wasn't too sure as they entered the rather dark entrance through a door that clanged as they opened it.

A small man dressed all in black came out from a back room, peering at them in the gloom.

"Uncle Solly, it's me, Mary, Mary Reagan." She raised her voice as Sol was slightly deaf.

"Mary, is that you? What a sight for these old eyes. Why haven't you visited more often?"

Sol's son Micah had died at the Front, and the news had aged Sol beyond his years. Mary felt a pang of guilt that she hadn't been to see him more often in the ensuing time.

"I'm sorry, Uncle Sol, there's no excuse—"

"Don't you apologize. I heard about your troubles— and who's this strapping young man?" Uncle Sol always got straight to the point.

"This is Daniel, Uncle, my fiancé," she said shyly.

"About time a good-looking girl like you was properly wed. Can I be so bold as to assume you have come to me for a ring?" he asked coyly.

"Well, yes, and no, Uncle. I'm no girl anymore." She laughed. "But Daniel has a lovely stone we thought it could be set and that would be both engagement and wedding ring."

Daniel pulled the leather pouch from his pocket and dropped the stone onto a square of black velvet.

"Oi, an opal! I don't often see these, I was expecting a diamond or sapphire, but an opal—dear, dear!" he exclaimed.

"What's wrong with it?" Daniel demanded. "I can

assure you its real. I dug it out of the earth myself!"

"Oh, yes, I can see it's real, and very fine, but opals are considered unlucky. I—I was just taken aback, my son." Sol could see he had upset the lad.

"Well, I think it is a very lucky stone," Mary countered, bristling. "It kept Daniel safe all through the war, and I want it as my wedding ring!"

"No offence, no offence, my dear. If you want an opal, you shall have an opal and wear it with my best wishes. Now to business, how would you like it set? I see it is not a cut opal, just rubbed."

"You know something about opals then?" Daniel was surprised. Not many jewelers in England would have seen them uncut. "I just had the rough taken off. I liked the natural shape of it," he continued.

"You know, Daniel, if it was cut and polished, it would have even more fire and be worth a lot of money," Sol ventured "And it would be easier to set."

"What do you think, Mary?"

"Well, its lovely as it is, but if it can be enhanced even more, then perhaps we should."

"Leave it with me a few days, and I'll look at it more carefully and have a few setting options for you," Solly said, turning the stone over and around, intrigued by the fire within. "There's only one cutter I would trust with this magnificent gem, but he does take his time. Are you in a hurry?

"We have a few weeks. Will it be ready in time?"

I'll speak to my friend and ask him to put aside any other work he has, as a favor to me. He owes me one or two."

True to his word, within a few days, Sol had several designs drawn out for them to choose.

Just two weeks after selecting the setting, Sol got word to Mary that the ring was ready, and she was soon showing off her magnificent ring to the admiration of all. With the expert cutting, the tiny pieces left were fashioned by Sol into a pair of earrings, which he tucked into the ring's box with a note, indicating they were a gift in memory of his son.

Those who thought the stone unlucky, kept their opinions to themselves. Uncle Sol had done a magnificent job with the setting, and Mary was sure it should have cost a lot more than Daniel had paid, but she said nothing, as it was probably a wedding gift for his lost son's good friend.

At Mary's insistence, the wedding took place quietly, with no reception afterward. After all, Daniel had no one, and Mary couldn't bear to relive the memories of her first wedding. After the ceremony, the two of them left for a small hotel up river from the city, where swans swam tranquilly between the trees that overhung the water.

Unlike Harold, Daniel was eager to get to the room and Mary was unprepared for him to almost rip the clothes off her body and push her down on the bed. If she had been expecting that Daniel would be as caring a lover as Harold, she was mistaken. He made love with the intensity of a man believing he'd never have the opportunity again. Shocked and bruised, she tried to rationalize it. Maybe it was the war, maybe the lack of previous opportunity. Whatever it was, she hoped it would not continue so brutally in the future.

They returned to Maggie's house the following afternoon. The weather was beautiful. Flowers bloomed in the parks, even along the railway embankments. Why couldn't it have been gray and wet as it so often was in England? Why make it so hard to leave? There wasn't much time between arriving at Maggie's and having to get to the docks. When it came time to go, both women clutched at each other, weeping noisily. Mary almost had to be pried away from a wriggly Joannie, who couldn't understand what was upsetting her mum, so she joined in the wailing.

"Come on, girl, time to get the tram," Daniel reminded her. "Don't want to miss the boat, do we?"

Maggie was desolated once they left. She was thankful she had Joannie, and the neighbors were kind, saying that it was for the best, and a year would soon pass.

It took a while for Joannie to settle down without her mother, and Maggie soon realized it was not easy for a grandmother to bring up a toddler.

After six months of endless worry, a letter finally arrived from Australia. The contents did little to ease Maggie's fears.

Dearest Mum,

I hope you get this letter, because I know you will be worrying. We finally arrived after six weeks. Some of the journey was very rough, and I was seasick much of the time. When we did stop, we weren't allowed to wander far from the ship, but it was wonderful to stand on land, even though my legs still thought we were on the ocean. You wouldn't believe the strange places we visited. I wish I could describe them more, but I haven't much writing paper. So next time.

Oh, Mum, I wonder what I have done. Woola Bella is so desolate, and we are living in caves underground because it's so hot. That actually isn't as bad as it sounds, at least it is cool. I have a kitchen, bedroom, and living room. The toilet is outside and we have to watch out for poisonous spiders and snakes. The isolation is so hard to bear. Supplies come in by waggon, but very basic. There are so few white women here and those that are, are rough sorts who actually mine the opals alongside the men, if you can believe it! Other than that, there's only the Aborigines, Abos they call them. They keep to themselves mostly, but I have begun talking to one young girl who desperately wants to learn to read—most of them can't. I wish I could start a school, but we have no supplies.

If you reply, please don't mention how unhappy

I am, or Daniel will get angry. He keeps telling me it won't be for much longer, but he hasn't struck what he calls the mother lode yet. I asked him if I could move to the nearest town, some one hundred miles south, but he said we couldn't afford it. Sorry to sound so blue, Mum. I am trying to make the best of it, and keep my spirits up, but you are the only person I can confide in. Don't worry, it's just another blisteringly hot day, and I'll get over it. I know Joannie is safe with you and, for that, I am grateful. Give her my love. I don't think I will be able to send for you and her as soon as I imagined. I hope she is not giving you any trouble.

Your loving daughter, Mary.

Mary's letter almost broke Maggie's heart, but it barely began to describe the hardship Mary was forced to endure. There was so little water in Woola Bella that virtually nothing grew. No trees for shade, and even when underground water tanks were finally constructed, she was only entitled to twenty-four gallons a week. Her friendship with the Aboriginal girl called Dee Dee, kept her occupied as she tried to teach her to read from the few books available, but it was hard going. Mary wasn't qualified to teach and the books were just incomprehensible shapes to Dee Dee. What Mary needed were children's picture books, but there was little likelihood of getting any. Dee Dee did know about pictures, though, and she proudly showed Mary paintings that she had done on cave walls and those painted by her ancestors dating back thousands of years. Mary marveled at the details and paint colors made from pigments in the soil and crushed rock. Through Dee's eyes, Mary was able to see beauty in the desolate landscape. She learned to tell the difference between scorpion and snake trails in the sand, what could be caught and eaten, discovered fossils on rock faces, and watched the sun change the color of the rocks as it set each night. Dee Dee might be uneducated, but she certainly knew about beauty and survival.

Weeks passed. Daniel roamed the outback, searching for his precious opals. He was often away for days at a time, and Mary, afraid of the men in Woola Bella, who were often drunk, made Dee Dee stay with her at night. They barricaded the cave entrance, not just to keep out the animal snakes, but the human ones too!

Eventually, Daniel would return and, if he had plenty of opals, he was happy, and would go out drinking to his success. If he came home empty handed, he would again go out drinking, but in a foul mood. Mary began to dread his homecomings, as his idea of lovemaking hadn't improved since their wedding night. When Mary became pregnant, it was obvious she couldn't stay. Daniel finally sent a letter to his sister Adele, asking her to take Mary in temporarily. When he got a reply weeks later, he arranged for her to travel to Adelaide on the new Trans Continental Railway and stay with Adele, who had been surprised to hear that Daniel was even alive. She and their mother were relieved but annoyed that he hadn't bothered to let them know and now wanting them to take in his pregnant wife!

Mary was terrified of traveling alone. Daniel came with her on the waggon ride to the station. It wasn't much of a station, just a tin hut at the end of the line. Waiting for the train in the sweltering heat, she and Daniel said their goodbyes. Dee Dee hovered in the shade of the hut. She'd walked all the way and was waiting for her chance to say goodbye. As Mary started to board the train, Dee Dee ran up and grabbed at her skirt. Daniel was about to shove her away, but Mary stepped back onto the ground and hugged the girl.

"Don't go missy, please." Dee's deep brown eyes filled with tears. It was all Mary could do not to start crying herself. Her one and only friend, and she was leaving her.

"I'm sorry Dee, I have to, for the baby."

The train whistle blew, and Mary could no longer wait. She gave Dee one last hug and turned to Daniel.

"It won't be for long. I'll get to Adelaide before the baby arrives, I promise," Daniel reassured her. Mary wasn't so sure. Daniel wasn't proving to be the most reliable of men. Probably it was his war experiences, but he was difficult and angry at times, for no apparent reason. Then he went off on "walkabout" not coming back for weeks sometimes, and she wondered if she'd ever see

him again. This was not what she had expected. Joannie
was stuck in England and who knew when she'd be able
to send for her and Maggie.

The train was full of very rough men, and she worried about her traveling bag containing the accumulated
opals that Daniel had found so far. She kept it held tight
against her, for fear that, if it was on the rack and she fell
asleep, someone would steal it. For hours and hours, the
train rattled on. The only relief was to walk to the bathroom, but what a hideous one it was. The toilet was a
hole in the floor over which Mary had to gather her skirts
up and squat with feet on either side. For toilet paper, old
newspapers cut up, and hung on a hook, but there was
nowhere to wash her hands. God almighty, she thought,
her journey outward to Woola Bella by waggon had been
preferable to this.

The journey was so long and tedious, the heat un-
bearable. And the train-often traveling through bush
fires—was always in danger. At the few and far between
stations, Mary almost fell out of the carriage to get to the
hut where she could at least wash her face and hands. As
these stations got nearer to civilization, there were more
and better facilities, and she hungrily bought a sandwich
and a drink from each.

Daniel's sister had said she would meet the train and,
true to her word, she was on the platform when it arrived.
Mary stumbled out of the train into the light filled, glass-
roofed station. The air was cool and she drank in the fresh

breeze. There was no difficulty in recognizing Mary—she was the only woman on board the train. As she walked unsteadily along the platform, Daniel's mother and sister came toward her. Almost collapsing in Adele Simpson's arms, Mary was hardly aware of being pulled into a carriage and driven along tree-lined streets to a white clapboard house with a somewhat overgrown garden. Once inside the house and led to an upstairs bedroom, she lay down and immediately fell into a deep sleep. Some hours later, when she awoke, Mary thought she was still dreaming. She was lying on sweet smelling white linen in a shaded room. Through the half-open blinds, she could see flowering trees and heard the muted sounds of traffic some distance away. It took her several minutes to remember where she was.

Getting up, she staggered her way to the door, calling out, "Hello, is anyone there?"

Immediately Adele came up stairs with a tray. "What are you doing out of bed?" she demanded.

"Well, nature is calling, mostly. Can you show me where the bathroom is, please?"

"Of course, but then it's back to bed with you. I've brought you something to eat and I'm sure you're thirsty."

In the bathroom, Mary ran her hands over the cold white porcelain basin, marveling at the bath under the window.

"Thank you, you are very kind and I don't want to be

a nuisance, but could I possibly have a bath please. I haven't had one in months," she called through the door.

"Of course you can, you poor lamb. There's plenty of hot water. Just call if you need help. I'll just go and get you some towels and a fresh nightgown," Adele replied kindly

Daniel's mother and Adele, both widows, were kind but still angry that Daniel would take Mary to Woola Bella. No white woman in her right mind would go there, and they couldn't forgive him for taking Mary, who had no clue as to what she was in for. Now that she was with them, they fussed over her, making her rest and eat wholesome food. She was excessively thin, and they worried that her lack of nourishment would have hurt the baby in some way. Mary devoured the fresh fruits and vegetables that were so amply available, and was soon putting on much-needed weight.

Mary and Adele became firm friends. Daniel's mother, though kind, was somewhat aloof.

Adelaide was a joy to live in, and Mary enjoyed all the facilities she had missed for so long. It was almost like living in London with the magnificent new buildings, but the weather was so much better and the walks along the bay were stunning. Most of all, she loved the Botanical Garden. It really hadn't been opened that long, not like Kew, but the tropical plants and trees grew fast in this climate. It was hard to believe the site had been a gravel pit and rubbish dump so little time ago.

Adele wouldn't take any money for her keep, so Mary determined that she would take the wilderness around the house, and turn it into her own miniature botanical garden. She didn't think Adele would mind, as she obviously wasn't interested herself. Once Mary had found a few tools in a shed, she set to work.

Seeing her from the house, Daniel's mother turned to Adele. "What is that crazy girl up to in the garden?"

Adele could see her from the kitchen. "Oh, my, she's clearing it. I'll go and tell her to watch out for Funnel Webs. She probably has no idea of how dangerous those spiders are."

Mary knew the dangers lurking in the undergrowth, but she felt she was well protected with sturdy boots and thick gloves, if only they weren't so hot! She was enjoying herself so much, she didn't hear Adele come down the path.

"Mary, be careful," Adele admonished. "Do you know what you are doing?"

"I know—believe me I know. I didn't survive Woola Bella without getting to know all the 'nasties' in this country. I was friends with an Aborigine girl and she taught me very well."

Adele wasn't sure what shocked her more—the fact that Mary knew about the dangers, or the fact that she had had an Aborigine friend. White people didn't mix with natives It just wasn't done, even in the outback.

Taken aback, she was temporarily at a loss for words.

"Well, I'm glad you are aware of the dangers, but you're pregnant, please be careful, and—it really isn't advisable to make friends with Abos, certainly not here in Adelaide.

"I'm sorry you feel that way, Adele. If it hadn't been for Dee Dee, I would have gone insane up there." Mary turned back to her gardening, her eyes filling with tears at the memory of her friend, and the way white people mistreated them.

"Well, fine," Adele replied huffily. "Come in and wash up for tea. Mum's set it out on the terrace as its cooler today," she added, as she turned and went back to the house.

Mary was to stay with Adele for over a year. At first, she didn't worry about Daniel's lack of communication, but as the months wore on and with the baby almost due, she began to wonder if he would arrive in time, or ever, Maybe he had died in the outback.

After an easy labor, the baby, a girl, was born, and Mary named her Kathleen. Still no sign of Daniel, not a letter, nor message came from him until nearly eighteen months later, long after Mary had given up hope of ever seeing him again. She began to wonder if she should return to London. After all, she couldn't stay with his family indefinitely. It would be such a wrench to leave this lovely place, the journey would be horrendous with a new baby, but there was Joannie to consider.

Daniel's mother, sitting in the front parlor one afternoon, just happened to look out of the window. "Adele,

Mary, there's a tramp coming up the path. Shoo him away, will you?" she called out.

Mary coming from the kitchen heard her and went to the front door. As she did, the bell rang. When she opened the door, the man almost fell in through the opening.

Adele coming up behind her shouted at him, "What the hell do you think you are doing, get away from here!"

"Adele, Mary," the stranger rasped as he fell against the doorjamb.

Mary took a second look. She couldn't believe her eyes. Daniel had arrived, dishevelled, thin, and unwell, but with a large bag of uncut opals clutched to his bony frame.

He was very ill. The years of living rough, following the deprivations of the war had taken their toll. Mary and Adele helped him upstairs. Mary removed his filthy clothes, cleaned him up as best she could, and got him into a spare bedroom. He didn't seem to have anything with him other than the bag of opals, so she simply covered him, naked as a jailbird, with a sheet, and threw his clothes in the rubbish bin. She'd worry about clothing him later. As Daniel was by now delirious and sweating profusely, they called the doctor. Upon arrival, he diagnosed Daniel as having malaria and malnutrition.

"Not much we can do for malaria, I'm afraid," he said. "The symptoms will come and go. Was he in the tropics up north?"

"We have no idea where he has been for over a

year," replied his mother stiffly. Mrs. Simpson did not forgive easily.

"Well, for sure he has malaria, but with some good food and rest, he should recover."

Daniel slowly recovered physically, but mentally that was another story. The flashbacks to the war came regularly, and he often became angry and violent, but mostly he just sat by a window in the clothes Mary bought for him, looking out into the distance. As Kathleen grew, and he recovered, he became more interested in life around him, and more like the man Mary had fallen in love with.

With the sale of the bag of opals, they found a small house to buy. Mary wanted to be near the ocean, and the house they found was just a short walk away. The small garden thrilled her, as there was plenty of shade, and incredibly a lemon tree. She hoped the walls around the garden would keep out the snakes, as she was terrified of them. Even so, she had to keep a close watch on the baby when she played on the grass—you never knew what dangerous spider or insect was lurking. Still, it was heaven compared with Woola Bella.

When Daniel was in one of his black moods, she would take Kathleen to the beach. While Kathleen and other children played happily, she would look out to sea, enjoying the fresh salty breeze, wishing things could be different with Daniel. Often, when she took the child back, Daniel was through the worst of his daytime nightmare and would be asleep. When he awoke, he couldn't remember the anger and violence he'd exposed his family to, and was his usual self. Adele and his mother visited often, but if only Mary had Maggie and Joannie.

Eventually, Daniel was well enough to work and found a job in an assay office, as he was a fine judge of the quality of opals and working kept his mind from wandering. In between his violent flashbacks, Mary couldn't really complain, life was wonderful in Adelaide.

The following year a second child was born and Mary now had a boy and a girl, but she still ached to bring Joannie and Maggie to Australia. When would Daniel agree to send for them?

She began to wonder if Daniel had ever intended to bring them. He wasn't particularly interested in his own children, preferring to be at work, but he'd always been kind to Joannie, if a little distant. Bringing the subject up usually brought on of his black moods and, eventually, Mary stopped asking.

Two years would pass with no letter sent giving Maggie the wonderful news that she and Joannie would soon be leaving for Australia.

CHAPTER 14

Joannie

Back in London, it was becoming apparent that Maggie was no match for the rambunctious three year old. The child was into everything, running away laughing when Maggie tried to catch hold of her.

Eventually, Maggie confided in her friend Emily Wyatt. "I just can't cope with her, Em, I've got the rheumatics so bad in me legs, but I promised my Mary that I'd take care of her. What am I to do?" she moaned.

Emily was younger than Maggie, was married, but with no children of her own. She went home to talk to her husband, Sid, about a plan she had quickly formed in her mind.

"Sid, you know I wanted a baby more than anything, and we never were blessed, but there is a situation that might be good for us," she told an unsuspecting Sid.

When she had explained her plan, Sid was not so sure.

"Well, I suppose we could see how it goes. Do you think Maggie will agree?"

"I think she will be relieved," replied Emily.

"But what if it's only for a year, won't you be upset when she has to go back?"

"I don't think Maggie will go to Australia by herself, she'd be too scared. Anyway, from what she says, I don't think things are going well out there and they are still probably stuck out in the wilds. I think we will have Joannie for a long time," she replied with a smug smile.

After a lot of persuasion, Maggie agreed to let Emily look after Joannie, fully believing that it would be "just temporary."

Joannie settled easily with Emily and Sid. She wanted for nothing, and Maggie had to admit the child was better off with them. Maggie visited but as time went by, she began to feel more like an intruder into the child's life.

Sid came to adore Joannie, and she him, but in the back of his mind, the niggling thought that she'd be taken away, was always there. Emily was convinced differently.

When, after a year, Maggie didn't mention going to Australia, Emily breathed a sigh of relief, beginning to

believe that Joannie was never going to leave and would
be with her forever.

When Joannie was four and a half, a letter came from
Mary.

Dearest Mum,

*Daniel finally got out of Woola Bells, and we
are all now in Adelaide. It took much longer than I
thought to find a place to live, and have enough
money to send to you. Daniel had malaria when he
got here and it took time for him to settle and be
well enough to work. The climate here is so much
better, and I can finally go outside and enjoy going
to town. We have a small house not far from the
beach, but you have to be careful, as there are always so many dangerous insects and snakes, and
there are nasty things in the ocean too. However, it
is so beautiful and the children, yes, we have a son
and a daughter as well now, are happy, and I know
they will love you and Joannie. The malaria that
Daniel caught in the tropics isn't too bad but he is
still far from well. I don't know if he ever will be
well. Shell shock is a terrible thing. He has mostly
good days, but then he gets angry, and we all keep
out of his way.*

*Now I can finally have you and Joannie here. I
know you will enjoy the warmth. I'm sending a
money order to Barclay's Bank. You'll have to go*

and check when it arrives, I hope it will be soon.

*I hope Joannie is behaving herself. She must
be so big now. I can't wait to see her.*

Your loving daughter,

Mary

Emily was beside herself when she heard the news
from Maggie.

"If you take her, I'll kill myself," she declared her
voice high with hysteria. "You can't have her, she's
mine!"

Maggie was horrified. She couldn't risk Emily harm-
ing herself, remembering how desolated and depressed
she had been, finding she couldn't have any children, following a miscarriage. Emily was a determined, if not
hard, woman who hated to lose anything, an argument, a
bet, even a hatpin. Had that miscarriage turned her mind?

Maggie couldn't argue that the child was having a
wonderful life with her and Sid, and from Mary's letter,
things were not that good with Daniel, and there were
now two other babies out there.

After several sleepless nights, Maggie made her decision. She would go to Australia by herself, explain the
situation, and hope to God, Mary would understand.
Maybe Mary would return to England and sort things out
with Emily, or maybe she would be content with the two
new babies and leave Joannie in England with Em. Maggie hoped with all her heart it would be the latter, though

it would break her heart to leave her granddaughter behind in England.

Maggie's decision stunned Emily, but she was overjoyed at the same time. Finally, she would have the family she craved. Life was going to be wonderful. Once
Maggie left, they would move to the seaside. Southend-
on-Sea was not that far from London, and it fitted the bill.
It would be just as she wanted—a family, a new start, and
a new home.

The money arrived at Barclay's Bank and Maggie
had to find out how to book a passage. Cunard's was very
expensive, even in third class and, not wanting to waste
money, she enquired at the docks and booked on a
freighter that took a few paying passengers. She was to
sail early in May.

When the time came, she approached Emily again,
but the woman would not budge.

Maggie sailed out alone with all her possessions
packed into two large suitcases. The freighter looked
huge sitting in dock. All the stevedores were busy loading
the crates that swung out on cranes from the docks, but a
couple of men helped her up the gangway with her bags.
At the top, she looked out over the East End for the last
time, feeling quite dizzy when she looked down at the
black water below. A man in a scruffy uniform took her
below decks to the accommodation she would occupy for
the next six weeks. Speaking no English, he managed to
convey to her with hand signs, that dinner would be up-

stairs at six o'clock. The cabin was unbelievably small, with two bunks, one on top of the other. She peered out of the tiny porthole, seeing that the water was lapping uncomfortably close, just below.

She was about to sit down on the lower bunk, hoping she would have the cabin to herself, when the door flew open and a flustered young woman almost fell in.

"Hello, I guess we're sharing then," she said in a heavy Scots accent. "Shall we toss for top bunk?"

Maggie could hardly understand her accent, but she got the drift, and was quick to say, "I can't get up there, dear, my rheumatics are too bad."

"Nae problem, then, I'll be up top. I'm Pearl, by the way. I'm going to Singapore to the Mission," she carried on, while unpacking and stowing toiletries in one of the small cupboards.

"Um, I'm going to Adelaide to live with my daughter. Are you a missionary then?" asked Maggie.

"Well, yes and no. I'm joining my husband, he's the missionary. Not sure what I'll be doing, but I hope I can be useful."

"I'm sure you will be. I'm Maggie, by the way."

With the tide coming in, the freighter had to be loaded and on its way. Eventually, the cranes swung back, and the crew prepared to depart. Soon London was slipping past as the ship made its way slowly downstream. As the river widened, the buildings became harder to see, and, by the time the boat got to the estuary, they could only just see the nearest coastline as fog started to shroud them. Foghorns blaring, the ship made its way into the English Channel. Darkness fell and the two women ate a plain but substantial meal in the dining area. None of the crew spoke much English, but that didn't bother Maggie or Pearl as they had each other to talk to. Both were tired from all the excitement of the day, and they returned to their cabin, hoping to sleep, despite the continual rocking of the boat.

CHAPTER 15

Too Many Husbands

Sid and Emily prospered. It was 1921 and having sold up in London, they found a house to buy, and settled down in Southend-on-Sea. Emily was the driving force in the marriage, quite the entrepreneur, buying and selling property, and making good money. She was also an inveterate gambler, but had modest good luck. Bookies all round Southend soon got wind of her successes, but she convinced them that she was just an amateur, and only bet small amounts. Without any horse racing nearby, she regularly took herself off to the dog track. After all, a race was a race, and a bet a bet. Sid found work he liked on the sea front, and, as long as Emily wasn't losing too often, he turned a blind eye to her gambling. They were living in an attractive Edwardian house facing the cliff gardens and band stage, with views of the Thames estuary. Joannie loved Southend—the river, the house, just about everything in her young life was perfect.

She was growing fast and soon attending school in an immaculate uniform, made by Emily. After school, she would wander down to the seafront to where Sid was working in a wet fish shop. Before long, she could name every fish, or cut thereof, on the marble slabs. The other fishmongers were fond of her, often giving a penny or two for sweeties.

On the way back up the cliff walk, she would stop at the band stage. It was a magical place to her. It reminded her of a wedding cake, the white metal bent and curled into ornate swathes, the glass panels glittering when the sun was out. If the caretaker wasn't around, she would get up on the stage and pretend she was a ballerina, twirling this way and that. The park gardens opposite the house were full of flowers in spring and summer, and, being a friendly child, she would stop and talk to the gardeners, who fostered in her a love of flowers and gardening, which would carry on all through her life. Sometimes one of them would pick her a bunch to give to Emily. When this happened the first time, Emily marched her back to the park to ask the gardeners if she had picked them herself without permission, even though Joannie assured her she hadn't.

"I told you, I didn't. Why don't you ever believe me?" Joannie wailed.

"I'm sorry, lovey, but I know how much you love flowers, and it might have been too much temptation."

"That still doesn't answer why you didn't believe me," Joannie replied cheekily.

"That's enough. We will let the matter drop, shall we?"

Joannie felt unfairly treated by Emily. It happened rarely, but she knew that Sid would never have questioned her in that way.

Every Sunday during the summer, there were concerts at the band stage, and people would come, paying to sit on striped deck chairs under the canopy listening to the band. Best of all was the annual Tiny Talent Contest held in July. Joannie would watch from outside the railings at all the children dressed in sometimes very bizarre costumes, as they paraded their particular talent. She would have loved to take part, but she could neither sing, nor dance, and besides Emily would never have allowed anything so common. Oddly enough, Emily did allow her to take part in the Fancy Dress Competition, and one year she took first prize dressed in a jockey's racing silks. Excellently tailored by Emily, they were very authentic, as was to be expected. Emily always bet on a sure thing! She had even purchased new leather boots, and a riding crop. No one else stood a chance!

Joannie however, did enjoy something else "com-

mon," but it was secret only she and Sid shared. The carnival parade took place in August, and she and Sid would
make some excuse to get out of the house, and walk
down the cliffs to find the perfect spot to watch all the
decorated floats, bands, and of course the Carnival
Queen, pass by. Afterward, they would go along the seafront to Rossi's Restaurant for an ice cream and then take
the open-air bus to Chalkwell Park and the Fair.

If Emily knew, and she probably did, she kept it to
herself. Otherwise, why, on many years, did they return
soaking wet from the all too frequent rainstorms on carnival day?

Horrifying news that the ship taking Maggie to Australia had floundered in the Bay of Biscay with the loss of
all on board was the news headlines in both England and
Australia. Mary thought Joannie had perished along with
Maggie. Why would she think any differently? She'd sent
passage money for both of them, and Maggie had never
let on that Joannie wasn't living with her or hadn't boarded the ship.

Emily, on seeing the headlines did nothing to advise
Mary differently. Joannie had forgotten and was blissfully
unaware of her "other" mother, and Emily never reminded her., Now there was no need. Life would continue
along the path Emily had set.

When Joannie was seven, however, her beloved and
doting "dad" dropped dead from a massive heart attack
while at work. Joannie was inconsolable. Whenever pos-

sible, she and Sid had roamed around the town together, and Sid always took his Box Brownie camera. How they'd laughed as he made her ham it up for a picture. There were many memories captured in the grainy prints.

Alone in her bedroom, she took a box from the wardrobe and tipped the contents out onto the bed. The photos fluttered out. There were so many of her, but so few of Sid. She found one, a bit out of focus and tilted. Sid stood grinning and mugging for her to take his picture. Sitting on the bed, clutching the photo, tears began to roll down her cheeks, splashing the precious print. Sid was the fun part of the family, how she would miss him.

Emily wept a few tears, then put on her practical face and thought about what she had to do. She was not a churchgoer, neither was Sid, but he had to have a funeral. There was a church across from the park and she wondered if the minister would perform a funeral for non-believers.

Well, nothing ventured, nothing gained, she thought. Putting on a dark colored coat—she didn't have black—she got ready to tackle the problem. Joannie was still upstairs, should she take her with her? She was still very young.

"Joannie, I'm going to the church across the park. We have to arrange things for Dad. Do you want to come with me?"

A small weepy voice called back down that she would stay at home. Emily went upstairs and, finding Jo-

annie face down on the bed clutching her photos, Emily's
heart softened.

"Sweetheart, I know you are sad, but maybe coming
with me to the church will help. You can choose a hymn
if you want and then we can go to the florist and you can
choose some flowers. You're so much better at that than I
am."

"I don't know any hymns and Sid never went to
church. Suppose the minister won't bury him!"

"Er, well, I'm sure he'll tell us what we have to do.
Ministers are supposed to be kind, aren't they?"

"All right, but if he's nasty about Sid, I shall kick
him," Joannie replied hotly.

Emily smiled. "If he's nasty—I'll kick him too."

The church was empty, but they walked in and felt a
curious peace. "I haven't been in a church since your dad
and I got married," murmured Emily.

"Why didn't you go after?"

"I don't know. There never seemed to be enough
time, or maybe it just never seemed important."

The minister lived next door to the church and having seen them from his study window in the manse,
opened the front door, and welcomed the two of them
with a smile.

Their fears were unfounded. "Come in, come in. I
know who you are. You're Sid's wife, and this must be
little Joannie. He spoke about you often."

"Pardon? Emily said. "Did you know my husband?"

"Not well, but I always bought my fish from him. He was so proud of his family and would show me his latest pictures of you, little girl," he said kindly.

"Well, you know why we're here, then. I'm sorry we were not church goers, but would you do a funeral for Sid, please?" Emily asked contritely.

He smiled. "I would be honored. All God's children, and all that! Sid was better than most. Now sit down and I'll ask my housekeeper to make us some tea. I expect she'll be able to find some biscuits as well."

"I don't know any hymns," Joannie blurted out.

"Well, I do, and I know I can find just the right one for Sid," the minister reassured her.

Overall, the experience of arranging Sid's funeral was not arduous in the least, even comforting. Emily and Joannie left the minister after almost two hours, relieved that Sid was going to get a good send off.

The sun was shining the day of the funeral. Sid's coffin had been resting in the front parlor, with an unusual bouquet on top. Joannie knew that Sid loved simple flowers, daisies, day lilies, buttercups. The florist was somewhat taken aback when Joannie asked for these, but she promised to do her best. The arrangement, when it arrived, was just perfect. Others sent elaborate wreaths, but Joannie knew Sid would be happiest with hers.

The funeral directors looked like stern blackbirds to Joannie, and she stood back out of their way as they solemnly carried the coffin to the car. Emily and Joannie walked hand in hand behind the hearse. Emily wore a new black suit, but Joannie refusing to wear anything dark, walked along in her favourite sky-blue coat—a present from Sid.

Sid had been such a likeable man, many of his friends from the seafront came to pay their respects and attend the service. Joannie sat in the front pew with Emily, looking round in awe. The minister, true to his word, knew some special hymns, and, because he knew Sid, the service was very personal and kind. Joannie stood at Emily's side as the wave of male friends offered condolences and patted Joannie on the head as they left the church. Emily stood stoically upright, accepting their condolences, hardly uttering one word herself and most of Sid's friends thought her a "cold fish." The sadness lifted somewhat, as mourners made their way into the church hall, and soon laughter was heard as they told funny stories about Sid, making Joannie smile. Emily kept herself busy, making sure the tea urns were kept full, but she found it difficult to make small talk. It wasn't her way.

After everyone had gone, the two of them walked alone from the church hall back to the house. How silent and cold it seemed, even though it was a warm day. Joannie shut herself in her room, taking Sid's old hat with her, and she fell asleep, tears fell soaking through it as she clutched it to her face. Emily, alone in her and Sid's bedroom, finally broke down and sobbed until she too fell into an exhausted sleep.

Money was not an immediate problem, and life went on without Sid much as before. If Emily was sad, she didn't show it. Joannie like most children got over the loss and was back to her old ebullient self quite soon, but she never visited the fish shops under the pier again.

Emily's passion, other than betting, was playing Whist. She was quite proficient and soon returned once a week to the hall over Garon's cinema for an evening of gaming.

She was well known at the hall, and people came up to her, offering condolences.

"Thank you, but we are here to play," she was heard to say.

A few gamers tsk, tsked to themselves, but that was Emily, hard as nails, except where Joannie was concerned.

One of the players she regularly partnered was a widower called Maurice Stewart. After what was considered a very short period of mourning by most people, Maurice approached her with a marriage proposal. He had three young children in need of a mother. He made no illusions that this would be a love match, more a mutual partnership. Emily weighed up the pros and cons. It seemed the pros outweighed the cons, and Joannie would enjoy having other children in the house.

Maurice was a pawnbroker, not a particularly well respected profession, but with times being what they were, an extra income would be welcome, and Maurice made a good living. Emily agreed to marry him. She'd always wanted a big family, and this seemed an ideal way to get one. Maurice was just an extra body in the house.

Maurice and his children, Grace, Eva, and Dottie moved in. Joannie was thrilled to have three big sisters, and all four shared the biggest bedroom at the back of the house. The youngest, Eva, was just a year older than Joannie, and they shared their dolls and toys, but, as was to be expected, there were arguments. Grace was the quiet middle one, the odd one out, really—too old for toys, too young to chum around with Dottie who, as a headstrong sixteen-year-old, was looking forward to being old enough to go out dancing at the local Palais. Dottie was always turning the other girls out of the bedroom so that she could preen in front of the mirror. The younger ones begged to stay, to watch her apply makeup which, if Maurice was around had to be washed off before she went downstairs, and to play with the jewelry Maurice had given her if they had little value.

Maurice, however, was not a particularly pleasant man. There were many arguments downstairs, heard by the girls upstairs. Arguments were usually about money, the lack, or the division of.

When tempers flared, Maurice would go out into the small garden where he found solace in his passion for growing prize roses. Emily had to admit he did have a talent for growing them. Every year, he entered his favorites into the Garden Show. He was never happy unless he took the blue ribbon and was working on creating a hybrid that he was certain would win this particular year. Despite the little garden being full of wonderful blooms, he rarely brought any into the house. Even Joannie, with her love of flowers, wasn't welcome in the garden. She didn't particularly care. She had the park, and his roses—all in straight lines, carefully labeled—seemed more like a science experiment to her.

After one particularly heated row, he was in the garden, when he accidentally gashed his hand on a pruning knife. Emily was in no mood to tend to it, so he just bandaged it himself, and got on with his pruning.

Within two days, he had a raging temperature and the doctor had to make a house call. After a brief examination, he made a telephone call and an ambulance whisked Maurice off to hospital. To everyone's surprise and no-one's particular dismay, he died three days later from blood poisoning.

Very few people came to the funeral.

To Emily's extreme annoyance, the pawnbroker business was willed to a distant relative of his, and all Emily got were the three girls! However, before the relative could claim his inheritance, Emily took the keys to the shop and quickly sifted through the stock, removing anything of value that had no possibility of reclamation later by its owner. Each piece had a small ticket with two prices on it. Maurice's purchase price was in code, which Emily knew how to read. The second was the sale price.

For just a few moments, Emily felt for the desperate people who traded in their precious items for so little. Taking mostly jewelry and small silver pieces, Emily quantified the knowledge that she was stealing with the thought that it was payback for the years of parsimony that Maurice had inflicted on her. Hard as she was, Emily would keep the girls with her. She was fond of them, Joannie adored them, and, after all, a family was what she wanted.

Emily again had to assess her situation. Eva, Grace, and Dottie had nowhere else to go, no relatives had come forward, and the heir to the pawnbroker business made it quite clear he was in no position to take on three growing girls.

"Girls," Emily announced at supper soon after the funeral. "You should know that I want you to stay with Joannie and me. Dottie, you are almost of an age where you could leave, but I hope you will stay. I'm afraid your father left you nothing in his will, something I will never forgive him for, but we have to look to the future, and I have a plan."

With only the one income, the house on the cliffs would have to be sold and a larger home in a slightly less prosperous neighborhood purchased, with the intent that Emily would open a boarding house. Joannie burst into tears. The house on the cliffs was the only home she remembered, and so many memories of Sid were within its walls.

"Joannie, I'm sorry, but there's nothing else for it,"

Emily said, as the three girls gathered around to comfort her.

"Don't worry, Joannie. We'll all be together, that's the main thing," Eva whispered.

In the autumn, a suitable house was found, and the cliff house sold. Their new home was in a row of ten identical buildings, just off the High Street, but it had six bedrooms, two of which were on the third floor, two more in the attic.

More bedrooms meant more work, and the girls had to pitch in after school. Dottie was now seventeen, and becoming a woman. She was also wilful and determined, much like her stepmother, so arguments were common.

Soon Emily had four men occupying rooms on the top two floors. There was a bathroom on the third floor, that they shared, and the girls were forbidden to go farther than their own second-floor bedrooms, especially Dottie.

By Christmas, there was so much work to do preparing a Christmas meal for all the PGs as the girls called the paying guests. Emily, as usual, was ordering everyone around, and the girls scattered to do their various chores. Eva and Joannie had to take the shopping trolley to Dorington's the butcher and fetch the turkey.

The girls enjoyed visiting Mr. Dorington and his wife. Mrs. Dorington had lost a finger in the sausage machine, and the older girls would tease Joannie that the finger was in the sausages, but when Emily happened to be with them, she scolded them for staring at the space where Mrs. Dorington's finger should be. This Christmas, Eva and Joannie felt very important to have to get the turkey by themselves.

"Ah, here's me darlins," called Mr. Dorington, as they pushed through the heavy wooden door, scuffing the sawdust that covered the floor. "I know what you've come for, and a grand bird I have for you. Mind I don't know if you're strong enough to push it home," he teased.

"Course we are Mr. Dorington, and Mum wants two pounds of sausage meat, three pounds of best stewing beef, and she said mind it is lean!"

"Would it be anything else, girlies?" He laughed. Emily was a tough customer, and he knew better than to try to fob her off with anything substandard. "You're looking a bit glum, young Joannie. What's the matter, love? It's Christmas Eve. Aren't you looking forward to tomorrow?" he asked.

"It's my birthday today, and nobody's said anything," Joannie said dejectedly. "I got no cards, no presents, nuffing."

"Oh, sweetheart, I'm sure it's because your mum is so busy. She wouldn't have forgot intentionally," Mrs. Dorington said, trying to comfort. "I have something upstairs for you. Just wait a minute."

Mrs. Dorington hadn't known about the birthday, but she felt so bad for Joannie that she went to look for a gift meant for her niece.

She'd worry about getting her something else later.

Joannie, unwrapping the box, found a pink cardigan with a white collar. "It's lovely, Mrs. Dorington, thank you so much. At least someone remembered," she sniffed, pointedly looking at Eva.

After watching Mr. Dorington wrap the bird and the meat, they heaved them into the trolley and made their way home.

Eva ran ahead and was down the front steps, leaving Joannie to bump the heavy trolley down to the scullery.

"Ma, Ma, where are you," she cried before Joannie had lugged the trolley in.

"What's up?" Emily called from the dining room.

Eva bounded up the stairs. "Ma, it's Joannie's birthday, and she thinks you forgot!"

"Oh my gawd. Quick get up to my bedroom and bring me the jewelry box."

Emily had demanded or been given, several good pieces from the late Maurice. When she heard Joannie slam the back door she called out to her. "Joannie, I've forgotten the cream for the pudding. Run down to the Co-op, will you? You should have enough money."

Joannie uttered a rude word under her breath and slammed out again.

When Eva came down with the jewelry box, Emily opened it to select a piece for Joannie. She was still a little young for jewelry, but Emily found a thin gold chain with a heart shaped locket dangling from it.

"Get me a box and some wrapping paper from the parlor, Eva. It's all in there, but don't look at the presents!" she instructed.

Joannie returned slowly from the Co-op, kicking at the leaves in the gutter along the way. She was in no mood to go home to the hustle and bustle of the house and the excitement of the other girls.

Nothing was said until the girls sat down to supper. They ate earlier than the paying guests did, eating in the kitchen. The guests ate upstairs in the dining room, but it was warmer in the kitchen and they much preferred it.

"Joannie," Emily said. "I'm so sorry I forgot to give you your birthday present earlier, but here it is. Better late than never, eh?"

The gold locket dropped out of the box into Joannie's hand. She had never had anything so beautiful and grown up. "It's lovely, Mum, thank you. I thought you forgot. Put it on me, Eva."

Emily breathed a sigh of relief. She felt awful that she had forgotten. There was no excuse, but it was such hard work running a boarding house this Christmas, as none of the guests were going away, and a full festive dinner was expected.

The girls had raided their possessions and hastily wrapped the items they had chosen. Eva gave Joannie a chocolate bar she'd been hiding behind the flour bin in the cold room. She was very fond of chocolate, and it was beginning to make her plump, as sweets were not something she was keen to share. Grace had found a pair of soft woollen mittens, and Dottie gave her a lipstick and rouge. Emily's eyebrows went almost up into her hairline on seeing the last gift, but she was hardly in any position to say anything.

"Thanks, everyone, I thought you'd all forgotten my birthday. These presents are smashing."

Disaster averted, Emily brought out supper and everyone talked about the Christmas that was about to begin.

After all the work of preparing the turkey dinner and pudding, Emily was almost asleep on her feet when she sat down with the girls for theirs. This time, they were eating at lunchtime, after the guests had been served. The men had eaten in the dining room, and Emily had been aware that one was watching her more than usual as she placed the food on the table. With plenty of food left over for the family, the girls and Emily were happy, and didn't miss the brooding presence of Maurice as they tucked into the feast.

Oscar Mawer, a prematurely balding man appeared older than he actually was. He was recently divorced, and his young son was unhappily living with him, as his ex-wife was overly fond of the drink. Young Alan was a sweet little lad, and the girls fussed over him, especially Joannie. A few months later, Oscar made his intentions known and asked Emily to marry him.

When Emily said "Yes," the gossips in the neighborhood had a field day.

Emily was well known, and the neighbors had wondered why she would marry him. She certainly didn't
need him. She seemed to have enough money, and he was
far from attractive, but Emily never gave them the satis-
faction of a reason.

It soon became obvious why the previous Mrs.
Mawer had taken to the drink. Oscar was an obnoxious
individual who quoted the bible while ranting at the girls
to do more and more in the house. When they began
working, the demands didn't lessen. He was mean with
his money, expected Emily to pay for virtually everything, take care of Alan, and fussed non-stop about the
girls' behavior.

Emily had made a mistake, but she was stuck with
him. His bullying treatment of young Alan tormented her,
and she took pains to keep him out of his father's sight.
As the girls grew older, they became more and more dis-
respectful to Oscar. They never called him by his given
name, talked back to him, and generally disobeyed him,
just to annoy. Dottie, the most outspoken of the three, de-
lighted in tormenting him with her behavior. She became
friends with a girl called Emma who lived on the next
street. Oscar considered Emma "fast," and she lived up to
that assumption. The two girls were often out late, at the
cinema or dancing, and when he asked where she was
going and with whom, Dottie would answer cheekily
"out" and "none of your business."

Eventually, all the girls except Joannie and Eva were

married and gone. Just the two of them, and Alan, of course, left. They were constant companions, taking cover from the constant arguments and often flying china. Mr. Mawer turned sixty-five when Joannie was fourteen. She wasn't particularly clever, hated cooking, and Emily despaired of her dressmaking skills. However, Joannie excelled at knitting, and once the teachers found out she loved to knit, she spent most of her time at recess knitting long woollen vests for them, and the occasional baby layette. Once she turned fifteen, she happily left school and started work in the Co-op bakery, where Eva had started the year before. Alan, a year younger, had to wait two more years until he could join the merchant navy, something he'd always said he would do.

When he went off to sea, of all the children, Joannie missed Alan the most. His voyages took him to exotic Asia, and even to the coast of Russia. Whenever he returned, he always had gifts for everyone. One such gift was a large chunk of amethyst quartz for Emily who loved the stone and had it cut into a large pendant, a ring, and a long string of amethyst beads that she wore constantly. For the girls, costumes from the Orient, beautiful silks, and Joannie's favorite, a small Russian bear carved from pinky-orange moonstone.

Later that year, when Mr. Mawer succumbed to pneumonia, all the children came home for a raucous wake. Emily was in her element. All the people she cared about were once again under her roof. It was the most fun they'd had in that house since Mr. Mawer had arrived. The only stipulation the children made to Emily was *not* to marry any more lodgers!

Alan continued to stay when he was on shore leave. Where else would he have gone? This was his home. Even when married, he and his wife Sarah continued to live with Emily. When and if, the first of the babies arrived, Emily would happily welcome the next generation. Until then, Sarah was good company when Alan was at sea.

It was so quiet in the house nowadays. As 1929 approached, two of the lodgers had to leave when they found themselves unemployed. When the *Crash* came, Emily took stock. She had never had any faith in banks, and, unknown to any of her husbands or children, she had quite a considerable pile of cash saved from her gambling, which was to tide them over the troubling times.

Joannie, still working in the Co-op bakery, was able to keep her job, though many of her friends were not so lucky. Eva, her husband, and baby had to ask shelter from Emily when Eva's husband Tommy lost his job. They settled into the house until times improved. Tommy made himself useful, doing repairs around the house, but he was devastated that he wasn't able to provide for his family. Such was life. Others had it far harder. Alan was still in the navy, and the other two girls were living across the country in the west. Their occasional letters assured Emily that they were fine. Grace's husband was a minister and Dottie's, in the police force, both well-protected jobs. People needed spiritual encouragement in these dark days, and others had to be controlled when riots, due to hunger, ensued.

CHAPTER 16

The Crash

Frederick felt crushed when he learned there was no money for university. He had dreamed of becoming an engineer or possibly an architect. His mother worried as he just moped about, following his high-honors matriculation from school. Poor Freddie, he knew it had really been just a pipe dream. His "class" didn't go to university, even if they could pass the entrance exams. Only toffs went "hoorah henrys" as they were often called by the lower classes. Scholarships were offered to poor nobility first, and if there was anything left...well, chance was a fine thing.

"Freddie, it's no use moping your life away," his mother scolded. "There's far worse off than us. At least we have food and shelter. Your dad works hard to keep his job at the bank, you know. You could apply there, I'm sure he would put in a good word."

"Thanks, but no thanks, Ma, the last thing I want is to beholding to him." Fred had little affection for his father, having watched the way he treated Maisie all his life. "It just feels that all that education has been such a waste of time. I could have left two years ago, but no, Pa insisted I stay on. What use are all those certificates going to be? I'll be lucky to get a job at the Co-op!"

"Just because you can't do what you want right now, doesn't mean you have to look down on other folks' work. You get yourself presentable and go look for something. I won't have you hanging around here."

Just because her heart was breaking for him, it didn't mean Maisie couldn't dish out tough love. She was at a loss at how to console her eldest son. Of all the children, he was the most sensitive, artistic, and prone to depression. Not being able to go to university was a blow from which she hoped he would recover. She wasn't even sure she was doing right, being tough on him.

Ernest had never asked his mother or brother for a penny. Even now when he couldn't afford to send his eldest son to university, he wouldn't beg. Colette and Robert had been in contact over the years, and he knew that Colette sent Maisie clothes for the children, but that was different. Letters from Robert told him about the factories, which had, surprisingly, survived the Depression, but

Franz was getting older now and looking to sell one of
the them, leaving Robert with just the one to run. Much
as he wanted to return to the family business, Ernest was
too proud and never asked his brother to take him on.

Each morning, Ernest still demanded a full breakfast,
and everyone had to be washed, dressed, and present in
the dining room. He would gloomily preside at the head
of the table, reading his newspaper until Maisie carried in
the food. Lately, it had been more porridge than eggs and
bacon, but it was always wholesome and filling. When
Ernest had left for work, the rest of the family would
scatter and get to school or work. Jack, apprenticed to a
builder, had an ongoing project. Surprisingly the South
East was still experiencing a small building boom, resulting from the bombing during the war.

Frederick, being out of school and out of work,
scoured the newspaper from cover to cover. The news
from the north and west was awful. Northerners were so
dependent on the mines and shipbuilding, but there was
little demand these days. People were standing in bread
lines and their hardship was desperate. Frederick felt
ashamed of whining about his situation.

As the Depression eased, the Co-op bakery was
where Freddie ended up, as a deliveryman. The work was
very mundane, but Freddie was personable and could co-
ax housewives into buying an extra loaf or a cake, so his
earnings were better than might be expected. One morning as he picked up the baked goods for his rounds, he

noticed a dark-haired girl with striking blue eyes coming off the night shift at the bakery. As she passed him, her aroma was that of fresh baked bread, more potent than the most expensive perfume in his opinion. She gave him a coquettish look with her blue eyes from under her long eyelashes as she passed by.

"God, she's a looker, isn't she?" he exhorted to his fellow rounds men. "Who is she?" he asked.

"Don't you know?" said one of his fellow rounds men. "She chums around with your sister. I've seen them out and about."

"Guess I've been too busy being miserable to notice what's going on under my nose. I'm going to ask her out."

His friend laughed. "Nah, mate, you don't stand a chance."

"You just watch," Fred replied.

Back home that night, Fred asked his sister Theresa if she was friends with a girl from the bakery. Theresa said she didn't know anyone from the bakery. *Surely, to God, it couldn't be Emma*, Fred thought. When Maisie was angry with Emma, she accused her of being just like her uncle Robert. Fred didn't think she meant it as a compliment. As it turned out, Dolly knew the girl from the bakery.

"I knew her at school, and we met up a while back. She's nice, but her mother is a right tartar, so you'd better tread carefully if you're going to ask her out," she advised.

The next morning, Fred made sure he was well groomed and presentable before seeking her out at the bakery before she left.

He was standing, trying to find the right words and the courage to speak to her, when suddenly she was at his side.

"Hello. I've only seen you once before. Are you new here too?" she asked.

"Y—yes," he stuttered. Damn, he always stuttered when he was nervous. What a fool he must appear to her. "I've just started and I wondered if you'd like to go to the Odeon on Saturday with me." It all came out in a rush, but she laughed and said she'd like to.

"What time will you pick me up, or shall I meet you there? That might be best."

"I'll meet you there if you like, and then if you change your mind, you won't have me standing on your doorstep like a lemon." He laughed. "I don't even know your name."

"It's Joannie Porter, and yes I'll meet you at the Odeon at seven.

On Saturday, Fred hogged the bathroom, annoying the girls intensely as they wanted to get ready for a dance. When he came out, Dolly eyed him up and down appreciatively. "Where you going all dolled up, then? Got a girlfriend?" she teased.

"None of your business, but as it happens, I have," he replied optimistically. Maisie pricked up her ears. "What's this I hear? Who is she, where d'you meet?"

Maisie was very possessive of her eldest son. Any girl he went with would have a hard time convincing Maisie she was good enough for him.

"Ma, it's just a girl from the Co-op. She's nice and we're going to the pictures. Nothing serious."

Joannie, at sixteen, had been out with a few chaps, none of which she wanted to go steady with. She was mature for her age, even though she was a couple of years younger than Fred, but he was quiet, kind, and seemed responsible.

Despite the Depression, Emily had fared pretty well, wheeling and dealing, and of course gambling. With the children married and Alan in the merchant navy, the house was too big for just Emily, Joan, and Sarah.

"I'm going to sell this house, Joannie. It's too big, and I can't manage it, now everyone's gone. I've seen a good property in Woodgrange Drive and, once this one sells, we'll move there."

Emily never consulted anyone, but in this case, Joannie was quite happy, as she would be closer to where Fred lived. Joannie and Fred became inseparable. They had an understanding that they would marry, but Fred wouldn't commit to a wedding date until he had enough money saved. Joannie was impatient, but Fred was adamant. It looked like a long engagement.

"We could live here, you know?" Joannie said, hoping Fred would agree.

"No way! You're ma is too interfering," he replied.

"That's a bit harsh." But, secretly, she had to agree.

CHAPTER 17

Changing times

Sylvie Mireille had passed away, and Colette felt her loss keenly. Franz did too, for she had been the backbone of the lingerie designs and with him since he was a novice factory owner. Colette was now the chief designer with *Soleil*, but she too was getting on in years. Franz decided that, of the two, this was the factory to sell. It was timely, as the early thirties were showing signs of problems in Europe again. A nasty piece of work called Hitler was flexing his muscles, growing the German army, and making threatening noises.

However, before he could put a *For Sale* notice up, he had to consult with Robert and Colette. Robert had become a strong, reliable heir to the family businesses.

He was running both now with good management teams, but Franz was adamant. It was time to sell.

"I absolutely agree, Pa. You and I both see trouble ahead, and, if it comes to another war, we mustn't get caught napping," he advised. "The East End docks will certainly be a target again. Both factories are now too small for armaments production, but we need to be away from the docks, not like last time," he cautioned. "Perhaps we should look at just selling the businesses, and you both could retire."

"Not sure I'm ready for putting out to pasture! But I know your mother would like me to slow down," Franz said, nodding to Colette.

"I agree that you should retire, Franz, but I'm not sure I'm ready just yet," she replied.

Robert cleared his throat. "There's something else. *Solie* profits are down this past year, and I don't think it's anything to do with the possibility of war. Our most profitable sales have been in New York, but lately the orders have slumped. I've been in touch with one of the buyers over there, and he tells me that it's cheaper to buy quality clothing made locally."

"Yes, I'm aware of what goes on in New York, but they use sweat shop labor and, of course, cotton is available from the southern states, which makes it far cheaper. I have always prided myself that *Solei Soie* is a business with good working conditions and fair pay for our girls. I will not lower our standards for profit. I would rather shut down completely."

"Shutting down will put a lot of women out of work, Pa," Robert replied. "Let's look at the situation in six months. I don't think we have to rush into anything."

Franz didn't get to talk in six months. Within a month, he died of a massive heart attack while sitting at his desk.

After the funeral, but before the will was read, Robert took his mother aside. "Ma, you know Dad left everything to you and me, but he never softened his stance regarding Ernest," he warned.

"Oh, I know that, Robert, but now he's gone, I have a few plans of my own."

The will was read, and there were no surprises except maybe a lot less in the bank than Robert had previously thought.

Colette prepared for life on her own. "Robert, I am retiring and selling this house. It's far too big for just you and I. As you know, Sylvie left me her house in the Mews. I wasn't sure if I should sell it or move in myself, but I think I shall keep it and find a tenant. If you want to continue with the factories, that's up to you, but I suggest you sell one of them as your father wanted."

"You're right Ma, I will be looking for a buyer for *Soleil Soie*. Maybe new owners will bring new life to the factory. At least I hope so. I hate to think of all the years we've put into making it a success to just let it go down the drain."

"Yes," his mother replied. "It will be sad to part with it, but rather that, than shut down. I couldn't bear to think of all the job losses."

"Where are you thinking of moving to Ma?" Robert asked, although he had a fair idea.

"I'm going to live in Southend so that I can be near Ernest and the children, even though most of them are grown up," she confided with a smile. "I think I will enjoy living by the sea."

"That sounds grand, but if you need a tenant for the Mews house, look no farther. I shall need somewhere, and if you'll let me, I'll be happy to sign the lease."

"Well, that would be most appropriate, Robert. Then if I don't like Southend, I shall return and live with you!"

"Yes, Mama," Robert replied somewhat ruefully.

Later that year, when *Soleil Soie* merged with a rival manufacturer, sadly, after so many years, the name of the company ceased to exist. Colette had already moved to Southend, buying a smaller Edwardian house on the cliffs overlooking the Thames estuary. She was glad she wasn't in London for Soleil's final demise. Franz had been so proud of his companies, but at least Robert was carrying on with motorbike production. Although the bicycles were still manufactured under the Robinson name, he had proudly named the new company *Leyh Motorcycles*.

Content in her new home, Colette's only real concern

was Robert. Now if she could just persuade him to find a nice girl to marry…

CHAPTER 18

A Lucky Bet

Emily, even as she aged, remained a gambler. Her favorite was the Irish Sweepstakes and, like most of the population, she would have a flutter on this popular horse race. This year was no exception, even though funds were tight. She'd had success with her gambling at Whist and the dog races, but she'd never won a penny on the Irish.

"Joannie, run down to the bookies and put a bet on Lucky Runner. I've got a feeling this year will be lucky for me and that horse," she said at breakfast.

"Oh, Ma, you never win the Sweeps. It's just a waste of money," Joannie replied, but she knew it was fruitless to argue about gambling with Emily, and she did win quite a lot on other bets. "Okay, I'll go on my way to work. Is there anything else you need from the shops?"

"Yes, bring me back some Nelson Cake from the Co-Op, if there is any."

"Ma, you know that Nelson is the bits swept off the bakery floor, don't you?"

"Never killed any of us and it's always a surprise what's in it, Anyway cover it with custard and your brother and sisters would eat anything. You shouldn't be so fussy!" Emily handed over some money. "Here put a tenner on Lucky Runner."

Joannie shook her head. Nelson Cake it would be and ten pounds most probably wasted.

Putting down rather more than she should have on an outsider, Emily and the rest of England anxiously awaited the race result. When the newspaper dropped through the letterbox, she anxiously turned it over and on the front page was the incredible news and photograph of the rank outsider winner!

Emily dropped to her chair in the kitchen. Unbelievably, she had won two thousand pounds, an enormous sum.

"You all right, Ma? You're awful pale."

"I won. Can you believe it after all these years? I finally won the Irish!"

"Blimey, Ma, are you sure?"

"It's here in black and white—Lucky Runner!"

It didn't take Emily long to figure out what she

would do with the winnings. As ever she thought of her children, even though none was actually her own. She sat at the table, doing some mental arithmetic. Each of them would get a portion, but Joannie, her Joannie, would get enough for a down payment on a house. That way Fred could stop procrastinating and finally marry the love of his life.

There was much celebrating in the house that night. Grace, Eva, and Dottie had all recently moved back to Essex, and everyone, except Alan who was away at sea, came to hear the news, overjoyed that they would share in the wealth. Fred was there too, but said privately to Emily after everyone had left, that he couldn't possibly accept such a sum.

"I'm not giving it to you, lad. I'm giving it to Joannie to do with as she wants, which I presume is to marry you. For God sake, Fred, make her happy and set a date."

Joannie needed her birth certificate to get a marriage license. She didn't remember her real mother, she was too young when she left. When she questioned her birth certificate name, Emily glibly told her they adopted her, her mother and father being dead. Joannie accepted this, as she had no reason to think Emily would lie.

Maisie had hoped it would be a much longer engagement and made her displeasure well known to anyone who would listen. She had nothing specific against Joannie, but cornered her one day soon after the announcement of the wedding plans.

"I suppose you're pregnant then?" she almost spat.

Joannie had inherited a sharp tongue from her adoptive mother and only replied haughtily, "Time will tell, won't it?"

Obviously, Maisie cast everyone in the same colors as herself, but she'd had a miserable life with Ernest and hoped Fred wasn't marrying for the same reason.

Of course, Emily insisted on making the wedding and bridesmaids' dresses. She still had the magician's touch with the sewing machine, and Joannie was grateful for the offer. Eva, Grace, and Dottie were to be bridesmaids, along with their daughters, so there were eight dresses to make, plus the bridal gown.

"I think we will go up to London to get the fabric," Emily announced. "There's not much choice here, and I still have a few connections in the rag trade, so we should get a good selection at a reasonable price."

That Saturday, the four young women and Emily took the early train to the East End of London. There was so much excitement, talking, and laughing, they nearly missed the station at Barkingside. None of the girls had been to London before, and had to rely on Emily's knowledge of the area, which turned out to be quite reliable. They found themselves in a seedy part of town, small shops squeezed in between dark warehouses, but Emily marched confidently down the street, stopping at one similarly seedy-looking shop front.

Barging through the door, she found herself confronted by a spotty faced youth that she didn't know. "I want to see the owner," she stated assertively.

"Not sure 'e's in; who shall I say is calling," replied the young man.

Emily gave her name and the lad disappeared into the back storeroom.

Quickly a more mature man appeared. "Can I help you?" he asked.

"Simon? Is that you? It's Emily, I used to look after you when you were little!"

"Blimey, Em! What are you doing up 'ere? I thought you moved to the 'sticks' years ago."

"I did, but I'm here to buy fabric for my girls' wedding outfits. Where's your dad?"

"Sorry, Em, Dad passed on three years back. The shop's mine now, but I'll see you right."

Emily was saddened, so many people from her past were no more, but she was thrilled to see Simon again.

"Right, let's get down to business. What have you got that's a bit special?"

Several hours later, after much discussion and bales of materials brought out by the spotty faced lad, the women made their decisions—apricot satin for the bridesmaids, pure ivory silk for Joannie, and of course as mother of the bride, something for Emily too. Everything wrapped, price negotiations made and accepted, the women, struggling with the bundles, needed a taxicab rather than the bus to take them to the station. Before the cab moved off, Emily suddenly changed the destination.

"Take us to Harrod's and step on it please, we're short of time," she told the driver.

"Ma, we're exhausted. What do we need to go to the West End for?"

"You need a trousseau," Emily replied.

"What on earth is that?" asked Grace.

"A nice nightgown, a slip, and some other items," Emily replied.

"Oh, Ma! I can make do with what I have. Don't spend any more money."

"Nonsense, anyway, you've never been to Harrod's. Every girl should buy something from there at least once in her life."

Joannie sighed. "I've got the horrible feeling it's going to be very expensive, but I'm too tired to argue."

The four girls' gaped open-mouthed at the imposing building in front of them as they stepped down from the cab. A liveried doorman opened the huge brass and glass doors and they trailed in after Emily, who seemed to have found a second wind, and was striding away toward the elevator.

"Years ago, the best underwear was made by *Soleil Soie*, but I'm not sure they are still in business. I'll ask the sales girl when we get to the lingerie department," Emily said.

Sadly, it was true, the company had gone out of business, but the sales girl was happy to show undergarments of a similar quality, she assured them, but from a different manufacturer.

"Silk, I think," Emily said, but Joannie put her foot down.

"No, Ma, that is just too extravagant. I prefer cotton anyway!"

The sales girl, probably disappointed that the sale would only be half of what she had expected, dutifully slipped their purchase into a distinctive green and gold Harrod's bag and the wedding party, exhausted from all the excitement, were soon on their way home.

Taking a break in the station cafeteria, as they waited for their train, they thirstily drank several cups of tea and ate the rather sad-looking sandwiches offered. It didn't matter. They'd had a great day.

The next morning, Emily set to work. She had never needed patterns, just a picture or a sketch, so, after Joannie had described what she wanted, Emily laid out the precious silk and began to cut. For the next few weeks, she was rarely seen away from her sewing machine.

Eventually, the pieces came together, and fittings took place. Once Emily made sure of the fit, Joannie wasn't to see the gown until it was finished. The four bridesmaids, and the little one's dresses worked upon, the wedding day was soon upon them.

Amongst the wedding gifts was something extra from Emily. All the silver she had taken from Maurice's pawnshop was still in the attic, almost forgotten. Just before the wedding, she had Fred get the stepladder from the garden shed and climb up to retrieve the boxes. What a treasure trove! Well, a stash of quite valuable pieces, and more than she remembered putting up there. Sorting through, she put some aside for Maurice's girls, and the rest she assigned to Joannie.

When Joannie came in from work, she found Emily busily cleaning all the silver, spread across the kitchen table. The acrid odour of cleaning polish pervaded the kitchen, making her gag.

"Blimey, Ma!" did you rob someone?"

How near the truth!

"Course not! I've had this for years. Thought it was time it saw the light of day. It's yours for the taking, if you want it."

Picking up an ornate solid silver coffee pot, Joannie snorted. "Can't see me using a silver coffee pot, can you? This is lovely though. If no one else wants it, I'll take it, but why on earth would you have all this fancy stuff?"

"Remember Maurice? Well I took it from the pawn shop when he died," Emily confessed.

"You're something else, Ma! What else did you take?" Joannie asked.

"Well, there's a box of jewelry too. It's all good stuff, but I'm giving some of it to Maurice's girls. Sort it out fairly., You can have first pick, though. It's on the side-board."

Joannie, not wanting to appear greedy, sorted the

various pieces for the others, as fairly as she could, but only took a large cameo brooch set in gold for herself. Emily came over to the sideboard to see how the division of the spoils was going and was surprised Joannie had taken just the brooch.

"I can't take fancy jewelry, Ma. I don't want to hurt Fred's feelings because he can't give me expensive things."

"Your choice, lovey, but I'm taking a couple of pieces and putting them away for you—just in case!"

"What do you mean 'just in case'?

"Joannie, I've lived through good times and bad, and believe me, when the bad times come, you need something put aside to see you through."

It was as if Emily could see into the future.

Unbeknownst to Joannie, who didn't trouble herself with reading about current events, Emily often had serious conversations with Fred, and they both agreed that another war was not out of the question.

"Well, I appreciate everything you've done, Ma, and I'm sure nothing bad is going to happen to Fred and me, but you do what you think is best."

Emily took a solid gold bracelet, putting it in a small bag along with a stunning diamond ring. Later, she would include a note in her will that Joannie was to have the bracelet and the ring upon Emily's death.

The day of the wedding dawned, but even on the day of the ceremony, Maisie was still against it—her reasons none other than she was overly possessive of her eldest—but she worried as he was still prone to moodiness and resentful that he hadn't got a career or even a good job.

She was dallying in the bedroom when Ernest called impatiently, "Are you coming, woman?"

Sighing, she put on her best dress, took out the pin curlers, and quickly brushed her hair. Her best shoes were going to pinch by the end of the day, and she wished she didn't have to make the effort to appear happy.

"This won't end well, I just know it," Maisie said to Ernest as she came downstairs.

"Why, for God's sake? They actually want to marry each other." He almost added "not like us," but held his tongue just in time. "Put a *smile* on your face, will you?"

All the Leyh clan were on hand for the wedding. With husbands, wives, and children, it was quite a crowd.

Emma had swanned down from London, clad in expensive furs. She insisted she was a housekeeper to a wealthy older man, but whom was she kidding? A housekeeper's wages didn't run to furs and jewelry. Her father knew exactly what she was, but this was neither the time nor place to get into it with her.

They took their places in the church. Fred was already waiting anxiously at the altar, with his brother Jack acting as best man.

"Have you got the ring, Jack?" Fred asked for the second time in as many minutes.

"For the last time, yes I have. Are you nervous, or *what*?" Jack replied.

Back at the house, it was time to leave. As the girls came downstairs, followed by Joannie, Emily stood with tears in her eyes. Never had they all looked so beautiful, and her darling Joannie was the loveliest of all.

Three black cars had been hired for them to make a grand entrance. The bridesmaids spread themselves between two of them, each taking two of the children. Joannie and Emily occupied the third, a Rolls Royce Phantom II.

Flying in the face of tradition, Emily was walking Joannie down the aisle. As they both stood at the entrance to the church, Emily turned to her daughter. "Please remember that everything I've done, I did because I love you."

Joannie was somewhat perplexed by this statement, but too excited to wonder why Emily had said it.

From the doorway of the church, beyond the fussing bridesmaids, Joannie could see Fred and Jack ahead of the sea of smiling faces turned to watch her come down the aisle. The minister, much older now, was the same one who had given Sid his send off. For a moment, Joannie was saddened. Sid should be walking her down the aisle.

The organ started the wedding march, and Emily turned to her. "Are you ready?"

There was no need to answer. Joannie's smile said it all.

CHAPTER 19

Fred's Decision

The newlyweds settled happily into their new home. Fred called his new wife Jo, and with her newly married status, Joannie became Jo to everyone. She soon made friends with another young woman called Edna, who lived across the street. It turned out both worked at the Co-op biscuit factory, but hadn't met before. Fred continued as a deliveryman. Jo was happy, but she sensed that Fred was unsettled. She hoped that, when they had a baby, he would be more content. In 1938, almost a year to the day after their wedding, Fred and Jo's son was born. Shortly after, friend Edna had a boy as well.

Fred was indeed ecstatic about his new son, James, and proudly showed him off to anyone who looked into the pram. A year later with James turning one, Fred came home later than usual. "Jo, I need to talk to you. Sit down a minute, will you?"

"But I'm just about to get the tea and—"

"Please." He began again as she sat down with a quizzical look on her face. "Jo, I know you don't take a lot of interest in what's going on in the world, and I love that you put our little family first and foremost, but we have to face the fact that Britain may be at war again, in the not-too-distant future."

"Stop, I won't hear of it," Jo shouted.

"Jo, we have to face it, and I've done something you're not going to like. I've joined the RAF."

This announcement met with stony silence, quickly followed by gulping sobs. "No, you can't, I won't let you," Jo cried as she ran out of the room and upstairs, flinging herself on the bed.

Fred followed her. "Jo, please don't cry. If war comes, I'll be called up, anyway, and I want to make sure I'm not conscripted into the trenches like they were last time. I'd rather die in the sky, than like a rat in a hole."

"Don't you dare talk about dying. How do you know there'll be a war, anyway?" she sobbed.

"I can't be certain, no one can, at this point, but I'm going to be away for a while learning to fly. I hope you'll be proud of me."

"What will James and I do? How will we manage? Where will you be?" she wailed.

"Come on, let's sit down and talk quietly about this, shall we?" he replied, trying to calm her.

Two weeks later, Fred's orders and travel warrants arrived in the post. He was to report to an RAF station on the border with North Wales. There wasn't much time for Jo to fret, and, all too soon, Fred was on the station platform, along with several other young men, all bound for the same squadron. Just like the last war, the women were left on the platform as their men, laughing and full of bravado, leaned out of the train, waving goodbye.

Jo, eyes brimming, stood almost riveted to the spot, watching the train disappear down the tracks, when a woman tapped her on the shoulder.

"Come on, ducks, let's get a cuppa. Not much we can do but make the best of it."

As Jo turned to see who had spoken, she saw it was an older woman, who told Jo she was waving off her only son.

"How can they go off like that, all laughing and joking? Don't they know what they are in for if it comes to war?" Jo wept.

"Ah, lass, it's because they can laugh and joke that makes it bearable for them, and for us. Come on, we both need that cuppa now."

Back home, the house seemed eerily quiet, even though nothing had changed really. Fred was always out on his rounds all day, but it seemed different somehow. A knock on the back door brought her out of her reverie. It was her friend and neighbor, Edna.

"Has your silly bugger gone and joined up as well?" Jo asked. "I've just come back from seeing Fred off."

"Mine just told me he'd been down to the recruitment office, passed the medical, and will be off in a couple of weeks!" Edna moaned.

"Well, misery loves company, so you'd better come in," Jo replied.

A week later, a much-anticipated letter arrived from Wales. Jo tore it open, thrilled to see Fred's familiar handwriting.

It was good news, and bad apparently. Fred started flight training, doing exceptionally well in all the tests, except one—eyesight. Before turning the page, Jo wondered why he would fail this. He didn't even need glasses. As she turned the paper over, she learned that it appeared he was color blind. With lights on the runway being red for "stop" or "go around" and green for "take off" or "land," being color blind to those two colors meant immediate dismissal from training. Desolated, Fred was not consoled by being put in a mechanics program instead. Jo, on the other hand, was elated. As a mechanic, he'd be based in England. It didn't matter where, as long as he wasn't in combat in the air or on foreign soil.

While Fred was away, training, Emily became ill, and the girls took turns looking after her. She had, thus far, refused point-blank to live with any of them, which was actually a relief—as, in her old age, she had become more and more truculent, often pitting one daughter against the other. It meant a trek for each one of them to the house on Woodgrange Drive, and the girls usually got an earful of complaints, so it was not exactly something to which they looked forward. Without consulting Fred, Jo finally insisted Emily sell the house and come and live with her.

The other girls, relieved that Jo had made the decision, pitched in to clear out the house ready to put it up for sale. Once cleared of all Emily's accumulated clutter, Jo called in Beard & Sons. They had a good reputation in the real estate business, and even Emily herself had a grudging respect for them. Mr. Beard's son arrived and, after pleasantries, got down to business.

"Unfortunately, with the war looming, there aren't many buyers, Mrs. Leyh. As you know, Southend is extremely vulnerable to attack. I recommend that you rent the house out, as you won't get a good selling price right now."

Taking his advice, Jo sought out a tenant, but it took a while, as more people were leaving the area than staying, and, when she found a tenant, the rent barely covered the taxes and maintenance.

Emily proved a difficult lodger for Jo. She demanded the big front room be converted to a bed-sit, leaving Jo, Jimmy, and Fred, when he was on leave, to crowd into the small back room. Even that didn't please Emily and, in one of her less lucid moments, she declared that she would be moving back to Woodgrange Drive just as soon as the war was over!

It became evident she was failing fast, but on one of her better days, she had delved into the sideboard to retrieve her will which she made Jo take to the solicitor. She wouldn't explain what else was in the package, just saying he was to make sure everything that was in it was delivered. It was all a bit cryptic, but Jo put it down to the ramblings of a dying woman.

Just after Fred completed his mechanics training, he got two weeks leave before going to his permanent squadron in Scotland. Jo was overjoyed to hear he was coming home. She missed him terribly, and he seemed to be having far too much fun with "the lads," according to the contents of his letters. Jo had written to tell him about Emily moving in. He was not happy to hear that Emily was enjoying the best room in the house, but he owed her a lot, and she was Jo's mum, after all.

It seemed like an eternity on a train from Wales and then the Underground across London to catch another train to Southend. It was going to be worse when based in Scotland, which was twice as far! Still, he doubted there'd be much leave once war was finally declared. The last leg of the journey, for some inexplicable reason, seemed the longest. There were other squaddies, who were based all over the country, on the train, every one of them anxious to get home. Southend was at the end of the line, and the carriages had emptied to all but a few people by the time the train arrived. As it pulled in, several men in uniform jumped out. Looking anxiously down the platform, Jo finally saw Fred, and it seemed to her that he walked with more of a swagger in his uniform than she'd noticed before. When Fred saw Jo, he ran, sweeping her into his arms, kissing her hard on the lips.

"Fred, really, we're in public. Put me down!" she gasped, but loving it all the same.

Fred put her down, and swung James out of his pram into the air. "How's my Jimmy then?" he asked, making the boy burst into giggles."

"Oh he's Jimmy now, is he?" Jo asked.

"Well, James is a bit formal for a dad to call his boy, don't you think?"

"All right, Jimmy it is. I hope you don't mind walking. We can't get the pram on the bus."

"No, I'll be glad of the walk. Seems like I've been sitting on the train for days."

The two strolled along, enjoying each other's company and catching up. Even though the day was chilly and damp, they didn't seem to notice. It was a much colder November afternoon when the two of them walked all the way to the seafront. Jo was horrified to see barbed wire stretched along the beach as far as the eye could see. Out to the east in the estuary, stood a concrete structure that Fred said was U-Boat defence.

It was beginning to sink in that Southend was indeed in danger.

Soon after Fred arrived home, Emily was admitted into hospital. Taking Jimmy with them, they visited her, and seeing the old, frail woman in the bed was a shock to Fred. Emily had always been a tower of strength. He'd had his run-ins with her, but he was truly fond of her, and Jo was going to be lost without her. It was obvious she wouldn't last much longer, and she grabbed hold of Fred's hand.

"Tell her, I did what I did because I loved her," she whispered deliriously.

"That's what she said the morning we got married," Jo remarked to Fred. "I wondered what she was on about then. Funny she should say it again." Jo was puzzled, but far too happy to have Fred back to worry about it. *Probably nothing at all*, so she put it out of her mind again.

Their two weeks together was soon over, and Fred was once again packed. They took what was to be their last walk together, for a long time, to the station. The two of them stood on the platform, with James well wrapped up and gurgling in his pram.

"I'm sorry you can't be a pilot, Fred, because I know it was your dream, but you can't know how relieved I am."

"Yeah, well, it just wasn't meant to be I suppose. I quite enjoy being an engineer on the planes. Perhaps after the war, my mate Les and I can open a garage. Take care of yourself and Jimmy. I'll write as soon as I get to Scotland, but I can't tell you exactly where that will be—official secrets and all that!"

This time there were many more women on the station platform, crying, hugging, and upsetting their children as they let go of their menfolk. Farther along the platform was friend Edna, who was also tearfully seeing off her husband. They came and stood together, watching the train chug out of the station, waving until it was almost out of sight.

The next few months were what some called 'the phoney war." Nothing happened. The bombs everyone expected to fall immediately, didn't. Months went by. The war seemed to be only in Eastern Europe.

Emily died shortly after Fred left, and, much as they cared for the old woman, it was a relief that she hadn't suffered too long. The family gathered again for the funeral, and the next day took the bus to the solicitor's office to hear the will read. No surprises. Everything was in order and fairly divided. The dour solicitor said he had a couple of disbursements to make on Emily's behalf, but it was her wish that they remain confidential. There was nothing more to do than get on with their lives, grateful to the woman who had taken them in and left her bits and pieces to them.

Months after Emily's death, a package arrived from Australia, addressed to Joannie. It had taken a circuitous route, with addresses crossed out and re-written several times. She and Edna were in the kitchen when the package fell with a clunk through the letterbox, to the floor. Curious, Jo went to the door and picked up the package, turning it over in her hands, looking at the strange postage stamps.

"I've got a package from Australia, Edna. I don't know anyone there. I wonder what it is."

"Well, you won't know unless you open it, silly." Edna was as intrigued as Jo. It wasn't every day one had a mystery land in one's lap.

Jo opened the package with great curiosity. She had no reason to expect anything from Australia, of all places. Inside was a folded letter:

Dear Miss Porter, or possibly you are married now and I'm sorry I don't know your name,

My name is Kathleen Simpson, and I received the enclosed letter recently from your adoptive mother Emily. She knew she was dying and needed to explain and apologize for what she had done.

Jo was intrigued. The other letter fluttered out.

Dear Mary,

I am an old woman, who did a terrible thing many years ago. Your mother was to take your Jo-annie to you in Australia, but I had been looking after her for near on three years because Maggie couldn't cope, and I refused to let her go. That was unforgivable in itself, but when I heard that the ship had gone down, I never let you know that Joannie was safe with me. It was a cruel, cruel thing I did. Please forgive me.

I'm so sorry,
Emily Mawer

Kathleen's letter continued...

My mother passed away soon after she got Emily's letter. She'd spoken about you when I was a small child, but after she thought you'd drowned in the shipwreck with her mum, she never spoke your name again.

If it's any consolation, you probably had a better life with Emily. Mum had a rotten time with Dad. He was terribly shell shocked from the war and disappeared on "walkabouts" for months on end, and when he was home, he could be violent. We haven't heard anything from him for eight years now. He's probably dead. It's easy to get lost and never return in the Outback. Please don't think too badly of him. He adored Mum, and she him, but he was so damaged.

You will find there's a little box in this package. It was the only thing of value that Mum really treasured, and I believe it should be with you, her

*first-born. I hope you'll write back if this next war
doesn't kill us all, as I'd like to get to know you.*

   I am, I guess, your half-sister,
   Best Wishes,
   Kathleen.

Jo was shocked beyond belief. As she sat in total silence, Edna jumped up, thinking she'd had terrible
news—but what could be so upsetting to her in Australia?

Picking up the letters, Edna read them quickly.

"Wow," was all she could say for the moment.

Jo came back to her senses. "Well, that's a shocker,
who would have thought—" Then she smiled. "Edna, I
have a sister, a real, blood sister! Well, half-sister, and a
half-brother! I didn't think I had anyone actually related
to me."

"Are you angry at Emily, Jo?" Edna asked gently.

"No, what's the point. As she says, if I'd been on the
boat, I'd be dead too!"

She fingered the envelope. It was lumpy. She peered
farther into the package, tipping it. A tiny box fell out.
Inside was a beautiful black opal ring.

"What an unusual stone, do you know what kind it
is?

"I think it's an opal, but it's a funny color, isn't it?"
Edna said, turning it over in her hand.

"I'll write back when I've had time to get to grips
with all this. I'd like to get to know Kathleen and her
brother—my brother!"

The following days the two of them spent trying to enjoy time with each other and their sons, worrying as the whole country waited to hear the response to Neville Chamberlin's ultimatum for Hitler to get out of Poland and stop his aggression. Finally, on the radio, they heard the news they had been dreading. The prime minister announced that England was at war once again at war with Germany. Like many, they sat in stunned silence, before hugging each other, fearing the worst.

Jo and Edna spent more and more time together, wondering if they actually were at war, and if nothing was happening, why their husbands couldn't come home. One morning, Edna, as usual, was in Jo's kitchen, watching the boys playing outside. She turned to Jo. "Did you ever reply to your Australian sister?"

Looking up from peeling the potatoes for lunch, Jo shook her head. "No, because I didn't think any letters would get delivered."

"Well, I'd try. You never know, and it was really kind of her to send you your mum's ring."

After a lonely winter, spring brought the war to England's doorstep with the sinking of the passenger liner, the Athenia, and then the Royal Navy ship, the Royal Oak. Britain was shocked into action.

CHAPTER 20

Separation

Edna came rushing in, banging through the unlocked back door to where Jo was making breakfast. She was waving a piece of paper that had come in the morning post. "Jo, did you get this as well? Are you going? Do we have to go?" she prattled.

"What on earth are you talking about?"

"This! It says we have to evacuate the children. If they are school age, they have to go alone, and if they are babies, we have to go with them."

"Calm down, and let's have a look at it." Jo read the paper thoroughly. "It's only recommended to evacuate the children, not compulsory."

"Do you think we should go? We're awfully near the

coast and the aerodrome is only a couple of miles away."
Edna was apt to panic, which wasn't going to help any-
body.

"I'm not going to go," Jo replied quietly. "I'm not
running. No bloody German is going to run me out of my
home," she said with more bravado than she felt. "What
do you want to do?"

"I don't know. It says we'd be billeted on a farm or
in a town inland. I don't suppose those people will be too
happy to open their doors to us, do you?" Edna replied.

"Right, we'd better find out what we have to do. I'm
sure the government will have a mountain of rules and
regulations we have to follow. I wish Fred was here."

Fred was not happy that Jo and Jimmy were not
evacuating, but he knew better than try to persuade Jo to
do anything which she had made up her mind not to. For
the next few weeks, the two women were busy getting
blackout material and sticking paper strips on the windows to protect them from flying glass.

Fred occasionally got leave, but getting back to the
south from Scotland was a big challenge as well as a
huge cost that he couldn't afford. Every penny he earned
went to Jo and Jimmy. With Christmas coming up, he was
determined to get home. An army truck was leaving the
base for the nearest town and Fred rushed to get ready
and be on that truck. It was full of like-minded airmen,
and Fred had to run and jump on the back of the vehicle
as it started off. As he leapt up and tried to grab the rear

half door, his foot slipped on the wet cobbles and he fell, smacking his head on the bumper. When he didn't get up, the lads on board starting hooting and hollering for him to stop mucking about. After a moment or two, one of them looked out and saw Fred unconscious on the road and blood pouring from a gash on his forehead. Given his injury, it was not a good idea to haul him on board or even move him, but the lads hauled him into the truck and ordered the driver to take him to the local hospital. Poor Fred, instead of spending Christmas with his family, he had several stitches put in his scalp and was kept in a ward for two nights, as he had concussion.

"This is a fine turn up for the books," said Les, his co-mechanic and friend, visiting him the next morning. "Trust you to get wounded without even being in combat."

Fred was still groggy. "What the hell happened, where am I?"

When Les told him, Fred wasn't amused.

"Not funny, I was supposed to be home. Gawd only knows when I'll get leave again. I haven't even been able to let my missus know what's happened. Why are you here? You're supposed to be home as well."

"Couldn't leave my mate with all these luscious nurses to tempt you, could I? Anyway, I'll get the train today. Just wanted to make sure you were okay. Jo didn't even know you were coming, did she? You said it was going to be a surprise, last I heard."

"Jesus, I'm sorry to muck up your leave, Les. Do us a favor, will you, if you have time, and get me some paper, and a stamp? I'll write and tell her what I planned, and what's happened. Don't want her to worry, but I guess I should tell her."

"Yeah, and tell her all about the medal you'll get." Les laughed as he turned and walked down the ward toward the door.

Jo and Edna spent Christmas together. Their boys, too young to understand, played happily together. Their mothers opened a bottle of sherry, toasted each other, their husbands, and wished the bloody war would end soon. By Christmas night, the bottle was half-empty, and once they put the boys to bed in the same cot, the two women polished off the rest. The first week of the year, the letter arrived, telling Jo about Fred's accident. She was relieved to hear that his head was healing and he'd be back on the job soon enough. He never told her that he was rushing home when it happened, didn't seem much point now that Christmas was over and done with.

The boys were growing fast. That Spring Edna and Jo found second hand tricycles for them, and they were soon tearing up and down the street on them.

At night, air raid sirens wailed often as Nazi bombers headed toward London, but so far Southend had been pretty lucky, just a couple of wayward bombs had fallen on houses, causing a lot of damage, but no loss of life. London was not as fortunate, as the blitz ramped up. The aerodrome near Southend was a major offensive base, and the two little boys were intrigued as the planes took off and flew low over their houses as they gained height to cross the English Channel. Jo and Edna didn't worry about the boys too much. They were at one or the other's home all the time.

When the sirens went off during the day, which was in itself unusual, Jo crossed the street to make sure Jimmy was indoors with Edna's son. "I guess the boys are in the garden, aren't they?" she asked.

"No, I thought they were with you," Edna replied, suddenly worried. "My God, where can they be?"

The two women panicked. The sirens were really wailing now as they ran outside, looking up and down the street. A passing air raid warden shouted at them to take cover.

"We can't find our kids," they yelled back over the noise.

"Right, I'll phone the police from the emergency box. You get indoors right now," he ordered.

Eventually, the all clear sounded, but there was still no sign of the boys. The two women were standing out in the street as a black police car wound its way toward them.

It stopped beside them, and they clung to each other, fearing the worst.

"I think I have something belonging to you ladies," the officer began.

He opened the boot of the car and withdrew the two tricycles. He then opened the back door and two grinning little boys emerged, each wearing a police officer's hat.

Each woman grabbed her son, smothering him with hugs and kisses, all the while threatening them with a good hiding if they ever ran off again.

"Where were they, where did you find them?" they asked.

"You won't believe this, but they were at the railway bridge, standing on the bikes, looking over at the planes taking off from the aerodrome!" explained the officer.

Jo gasped. "But that's a good three miles away!"

"You're right, there. Better put a leash on these lads," he admonished with a smile.

That was the first of many escapades the boys got up to over the next few years.

Fred wrote often and, in one of his letters, he enclosed a postal order for seven pounds, telling Jo it was to buy the materials for an Anderson air raid shelter, as he was worried about her staying in the house during a raid, which he felt was sure to happen sooner rather than later.

"Waste of money, I call it," she remarked to Edna over their morning cuppa together. "What if the bomb falls on it—can't see it'll save us any more than the house will." They were looking over a pamphlet she'd found at the post office, called "Constructing an Anderson Shelter."

"Well, you'd better get the stuff, or Fred will be mad.

We can both use it—at least we'll be together. How are we going to dig that deep, though, and sling all that mud on top of it?"

"Beats me. Let's hope the lads get some leave and come home to help."

When a delivery truck dumped a pile of pre-cut corrugated metal, struts, nuts, and bolts in the back garden, the two women looked at each other in dismay.

"How are we supposed to build this?" they asked of the man delivering the shelters.

"Not that 'ard, if yer fit. But yer got ter dig the 'ole first. Any lads left round 'ere? They might give you an 'and."

Edna and Jo looked at each other as he left. "We'll have to do something or the boys will be climbing all over it and getting hurt. Give us a look at those plans again. We're not daft. We'll do it—be our war effort, won't it?" they said, laughing.

Taking advantage of a spell of dry weather the next morning, the women got to work on the hole. "Why can't it sit on the ground? Jo asked, being tired of digging already.

"Dunno, but it says dig down at least a foot, so we'd better do it right.

Arthur Wakefield from next door was leaning on his fence, watching with amusement. "I'm too old to put up one of these contraptions. Better to die in my bed."

"Let's hope we only have to use it as a garden shed,

Arthur. Be useful after the war, won't it?"

Arthur chuckled his way back into the house, shaking his head.

They got back to work, hampered by the boys playing with the various small parts, especially when the women needed them. Eventually, after a lot of grunting and groaning, the hut was up, and the two boys romped inside.

Jo shivered. "How are we going to keep it dry? It feels damp already."

"We'll have to put some boards down on the floor. I'll see what we have in our shed," Edna replied.

She hardly had the words out of her mouth when Arthur came shuffling up to the fence again. "You'll need boards on the floor," he advised. "I got some down the end. Come over and see if any are the right size."

Jo stayed with the boys while Edna headed down Arthur's overgrown garden. She came back triumphantly carrying as many boards as she could lift. "He's got enough down there for the whole floor. Put these down and I'll get the rest."

Arthur was back on his leaning spot.

"Thanks, Arthur," Jo said. "When we've got it all cozy, we'll invite you in for tea."

He grinned. "Hrmmph! I'll take the tea in the kitchen if it's all the same to you."

Over the next few days, a rag-tag assortment of equipment made its way into the hut, but it would never be exactly cozy. They hoped they'd never have to use it.

Jo's days were taken up with finding enough food to keep a growing boy and herself fed. The day Edna rushed home and said the Co-op had oranges, Jo went as quickly as she could to get her ration of them. It had been so long since there had been any citrus fruit. Jimmy didn't really like the powdered orange she made him drink so that he'd have some vitamin C. Standing in line, she hoped she wasn't too late. Finally, she made her way to the front of the queue, only to find one wizened piece of fruit left.

Jimmy looked at the orange, asking what it was. He couldn't remember ever having eaten one in his young life.

"It's an orange, Jimmy. You'll like it."

"Looks funny. I don't want it."

"Oh, Jimmy, look, I'll squeeze the juice out, then you can taste it, all right?"

Jimmy took a small sip of the juice, and, then with a grin, gulped it all down. Sadly, it came up again as quickly as it went down when Jimmy threw up the juice and whatever else he'd had that day, all over the kitchen floor.

"Told you I didn't want it," he cried as he sped upstairs before he could get into any more trouble.

When Jo told Edna, the two of them had to laugh. If they didn't, they'd probably cry. They really shouldn't grumble about the rationing and shortages. God only knew what was going on across the Channel and now, virtually, the whole world. However, the nighttime got them down. It was so lonely with the men gone. Jo hadn't been married very long, and for half of it she'd been carrying Jimmy. She felt like she'd had no love life at all and would be too old, by the time the war ended and Fred came home. Writing to Fred wasn't much help. She got the feeling he was quite happy in the RAF, even if he was only a mechanic and not the pilot he had dreamed of being. If only he could get leave.

When Fred wrote home, he always tried to sound cheerful. He didn't want to worry Jo. The reality of his life was somewhat different. Technically just a mechanic, he never wrote home of the times he rushed out to a crash-landed plane or pulled dead or terribly injured crewmen out the flames. It was sickening, something he wanted to never think or talk to anyone about. They were all in the same boat, he and his mates. The only way to deal with it was to spend time at the pub, drinking and laughing, putting it out of their minds. Occasionally, one of the lads would go off with a pretty girl, to the hoots and whistles of those left at the bar. Fred was tempted— he was a man, after all, and it had been so long since he and Jo had been together.

He was good friends with Les, and they confided in each other as they bemoaned their lack of a love life. It was 1942, after all, and they'd been away since 1939.

"How much longer till we get some leave, Les? If I'm tempted, what if Jo is? There's a lot of Yanks in Southend now, and you know what they're like."

Whether they actually did know what the Yanks were like or just surmised, thinking they had the same urges as themselves, no one actually knew. Still, they needed to get home and make sure everything was as it should be.

Another dark dawn broke during the Scottish winter. The men rose from their bunks, shivering. The damned oil stove had gone out again. This was no time to be fussy about their ablutions. They threw on their work coveralls and great coats, and ran slipping across the icy roadway to the mess hut. Sarge took one look at their unshaven faces, rolled his eyes, and got on with what he had to say.

"Little, Leyh, Warren, Smith—you all got a week's leave, starting tomorrow. Collect your travel warrants, and good luck to you getting out of this hellhole!"

Fred and Les turned to each other, grinning, clapping each other on the back. It had been so long since they'd had leave. Warren and Smith were lucky they only had to get to the Midlands. Fred and Les both caught the train to London, where they parted company. Les had to get to Watford in Hertfordshire, and Fred, having farther to go, hotfooted it to Liverpool Street Station and a connection to Southend. With no time to warn Jo he was coming, he was sure she'd be happy with the surprise visit. It was so good to be back. London, poor battered London, was a wonderful sight to see. Arriving at Euston Station, Fred walked to Liverpool Street where he would make the connection to Southend. Looking at St. Paul's still standing proud, he thought, *If that goes, we're done for*. However how the Germans could miss it was incredible. It was such a huge landmark.

Trains were infrequent these days, but he was happy just to soak up the sights and sounds of the old station. Even the weather was better, as a watery sun poked through the cloud, shining over the ruins of the East End docks. Finally, he boarded the train, which pulled slowly away. Was it his imagination, or was the train moving much slower than before?

At last, he arrived at Southend Victoria Station and, slinging his kitbag over his shoulder, started walking home. Home—what a wonderful ring that word had to it. As he walked, he started thinking. Jimmy was six now. Would he remember him? He hadn't seen him for three years. *That's a long time for a kiddie*. He wished he had a present for his boy, but as he passed the shops in the High Street, there was little in the windows and nothing that looked like it might please a six-year-old. Every street, every tree, every house was familiar. Eventually, he turned into their street and saw the house he and Jo had so lovingly chosen what seemed like an eternity ago. Edna was standing at his front gate, looking over and talking to someone he couldn't see. As he came closer, she turned and gasped. "Fred, it's you!"

Jo leapt up, from weeding the vegetable patch, almost banging into Edna. "Oh my, it is you, and I look awful. Why didn't you tell me you were coming?" she wailed as tears started down her cheeks.

"You couldn't look awful if you tried." Fred beamed. "And there wasn't any time. I didn't find out until yesterday!"

"Yesterday? You've been traveling all night? Come on let's get inside. Sorry, Edna, I'll see you later."

"Guess you'll be wanting a baby sitter then," Edna remarked coyly.

"Wouldn't say no, Edna love," Fred replied with a grin.

Jimmy came running up to see who the strange man in uniform was. Fred knelt down and held his arms out, but Jimmy held back.

"It's your dad, Jimmy," Jo said. "He's come all this way to see you, give him a hug."

Jimmy wasn't so sure, but he did as he was told. Fred swung him up in the air and twirled him around. If Jimmy wasn't sure who he was, he looked like he might be fun to have around, so locking his arms around Fred's neck, he laughed and demanded he do it again.

It was as if they'd been apart forever, and neither wanted the week to end, but they both knew it must.

"It's so lonely without you, Fred. I imagine all sorts of things. I worry that you'll get hurt again, that you'll fall for a pretty Scottish girl—can't you get transferred nearer home?"

"I don't think my wanting to transfer is top of the war department's priorities," he said with a laugh. Suddenly serious, he added, "I feel just the same about you, with the Yanks in town, or that you'll get bombed, but I promise I won't look at another woman. I have the best waiting here for me. I do have that, don't I? One day this nightmare will end, I promise. Now show me this Anderson shed and all the veggies you're growing," he added gruffly, clearing his throat.

All too soon, Fred's leave was over, and Jo was once again at the train station, watching and waving as the train chugged out of sight.

CHAPTER 21

Winslow

Once again, Fred was on the train back to Scotland. The journey, no better or worse than the one heading south, seemed even longer, darker, and drearier. Wasn't that always the way with return journeys, unless the return was to home? Tired and dirty after two days of travel, he was in no mood for the kidding around that he faced upon opening the barrack door.

"So the wanderer returns! Catch up with the missus? Set another pot to boil?" such was the chorus of bawdy jokes that met him.

"Leave it out, lads, I'm bushed," Fred replied, falling onto his bunk and closing his eyes.

Les laughed. "No rest for the wicked, mate. You're to

report to the wing commander soon as you get in—at the double soldier!"

"You're kidding! What for?"

"Don't ask me, p'raps he wants you to take over from him, ha, ha!"

Wrapping his great coat around him again against the biting wind and stinging sleet, Fred crossed the quad and rapped, probably a bit too loudly, on the wing commander's door.

"Ah, Leyh, good to see you back, but it looks like I'm losing you," the commander said, wasting few words. "I've been watching you, lad, and I checked up with HQ. Seems you're quite a bright spark from your matriculation results! Thought you might have gone on to university, eh?"

"Not much chance of that in 1929, sir," Fred replied. What the devil was going on?

"I know you were disappointed about the pilot training, but I had a word with the MOD, and they want to see you about 'special' training."

"What sort of 'special training,' sir?"

"Can't tell you, old chap, official secrets, and all that. Here are your travel warrants. You're to report to a place called Winslow House. Bit nearer home for you, I think—if you get any leave, that is. Anyway, get your head down, and leave tomorrow morning. And, mum's the word, lad."

Back at the hut, the squaddies were full of questions.

Fred, as ignorant of what was going on as they and, sworn to secrecy, could only say he was being transferred down south and had to leave in the morning.

"Lucky bugger! Wouldn't mind getting away from this wilderness myself," said Les ruefully. "Where you transferred to, then?"

"Sorry, Les, not allowed to say. I'm in the dark as much as you. We'll keep in touch, though, eh?" Lying down on his cot, Fred turned away, hoping to sleep, but tossed and turned for hours before finally closing his eyes. *Back on that bloody train* were his last thoughts before drifting off.

There had been no missions overnight, the weather had been too bad, and it wasn't letting up as dawn broke. After a quick breakfast and saying goodbye to the lads, Fred loaded his kitbag onto a waiting lorry and headed, for the last time, to the little Scottish station with its single rail line. Chugging into Edinburgh, the train reached its destination. A quick cuppa at the station buffet was all Fred had time for before boarding the so-called express to Luton. These days there were no express trains, and every few miles the train drew into some local station, more often than not picking up soldiers returning from leave. By the time it reached Luton, the train was packed with men in damp overcoats and kitbags. Not many got off there, which was the nearest station to his destination, and Fred, not knowing the area, was stumped as to how he'd get to this Winslow place.

Blinking in the sudden bright sunshine beaming through the glass roof over the platform, he handed over his ticket to the stationmaster and was more than surprised when, outside the booking hall, a girl addressed him by name and indicated he should follow her to a waiting car.

"I'm Vi, sir, your driver. Let me take your bag," she said, grabbing his kit and swinging it into the open car boot. She then opened the rear door of the car and indicated he should get in.

"I'm being chauffeured? This is all very odd. Can you tell me anything about where I'm going, Vi?" he asked politely.

"Best not, sir. You'll be briefed as soon as we arrive, and then shown to your quarters. Truth be known, sir, I don't know exactly what goes on either. Are you hungry? There's box next to you with sandwiches and a drink. Nothing special, I'm afraid."

After months in the raw and barren Scottish highlands, Fred had almost forgotten how green and lush the English countryside was. The car was winding its way along narrow country lanes, along which nearly every field was growing some sort of foodstuff. There were very few animals in the meadows these days. Mostly, they were turned over to wheat growing. Dairy herds still survived, as milk was vital for the children, but no sheep or goats. Who knew they gave too little meat for the fodder they consumed? He would have to savor the last roast lamb dinner he'd had at the pub in Scotland. At least, up there, sheep still roamed the hills.

After ravenously eating the meat paste sandwiches washed down with the bottle of cider, exhaustion overtook him, and he fell asleep. He woke as the car stopped suddenly, and voices outside were demanding passes.

Vi laughed. "You know who I am, Bob. I only left a few hours ago, and I've got the new recruit."

"No laughing matter, Vi. You know the rules and I need to see his documents anyway," the soldier on duty replied.

"All right, keep your hair on." Turning to Fred, Vi asked for his papers.

Once the soldier was satisfied, Vi drove through the iron gates, along a tree-lined drive, to an imposing red brick house almost concealed behind trees and overgrown rhododendron bushes in full spring bloom.

"Welcome to Winslow House, soldier. Go in, someone will get you sorted," Vi said, dumping his kitbag out of the car. "See you around."

Pushing open the imposing oak door, Fred stood looking around the entrance hall of what he assumed was a manor house. A rather shabby utility type desk and chair had been placed beside the grand staircase, but nobody occupied the seat. It was deathly quiet. Fred had begun to wonder if there'd been some almighty cock up, when a young man wearing civvies and puffing a pipe came bouncing down the stairs.

"Sorry, old chap, leaving you hanging like that, but welcome anyway. We only go by first names here, so I'm Cyril, and you are Fred, right? I expect you're wondering what's going on, so let me take you through to meet the gaffer."

"Is this a civilian unit or something?" asked Fred.

"MOD actually, and top secret, so no chatting up the locals, not that we get out much."

It was a short walk to the to the "gaffer's" office. Fred wasn't sure what a "gaffer" was, but it turned out to be the boss of whatever went on here.

"Ah, Fred, there you are. Been expecting you and I'm sure you've got a hundred questions, so let's get on, and I'll answer as many as I can." Rocking back on his chair, the gaffer took a pipe from the desk and began filling it. Failing to find a match he looked expectantly at Fred, who dove into his pocket to find a box of matches. "Thanks, old chap," the gaffer said as clouds of blue smoke enveloped his head. "As you've heard, we only go by first names here, and I'm known by one and all as Gaffer." He paused as a coughing fit overtook him. Spluttering he carried on. "Winslow, as I'm sure you've gathered, is a top secret location where we are working on code breaking amongst other things. We have top-notch men and women working here, and you're to join them. Fresh eyes and brains as it were. I know you haven't any experience, but then neither had any of us initially. You're mathematically gifted, but didn't get to go to university. Why was that?"

"Um, it was 1929, sir, and I had no way of paying the tuition, let alone the accommodation."

"Right, right, well then, this is your opportunity. How far you go is up to you. It doesn't end here. Once this damned war is over, the technology we're using now will be just the start."

All through the one-sided conversation, Fred sat open mouthed in awe. He was amazed at how much they knew about him, what he was going to do, how he was going to help. Was he dreaming?

"Now, I'll get Cyril back in to take you to your billet and show you around. Some areas are off limits, even to me! Welcome aboard, I know you'll be an asset to us."

Fred wondered how on earth he could be *any* help, let alone an asset, but this was incredible, a chance to make something of himself as he'd always dreamed.

Cyril reappeared. They walked through corridors, hearing muted sounds coming from behind the shut doors. Cyril gave a non-stop monologue as to how to live at Winslow until Fred thought his head would explode. Eventually, they turned into a room with French doors opening out to the rear of the house. What occupied the grounds was unbelievable. It looked like a small town! Row upon row of green painted single storey huts as far as they eye could see.

"Okay, you're in Block B, hut fifteen. Let's get your

gear stowed, and, as it's coming up supper time, we'll head to your mess hall."

The following days were a nightmare of frustration. Getting lost was one of the issues, feeling totally out of his depth was another, but eventually Fred settled into the routine as the thousands of others had. It was odd not to talk about the work with anyone in any other section than your own. So high was security, Fred had to get permission to write to Jo, and, even then, his letters had to pass the censor. All he could tell her was he'd transferred to a base nearer home, but not where it was or what he was doing. Her letters to him had to be addressed to a post office box.

Chapter 22

1945 ~The End

When Fred was transferred to England, Jo immediately thought he'd get more leave, or if not more, at least it would be easier for him to get home. She had been bitterly disappointed and confused when his first letter arrived. Whatever was going on?

When he finally got a few days leave, he seemed so different—almost as if he had to think about every word he said to her, before he said it.

"Jo, I know I'm being mysterious, but I just can't give you any details. Just know that I'm doing something for the war, and I had to take the official secrets oath. They sought me out, and I hope it'll be an opportunity for us after the war. Please don't tell anyone even the little I've told you—promise?"

"Well, I'm glad you are doing something you enjoy, and of course I'll keep it to myself, but can't you just relax a bit more? You seem so distant and Jimmy needs to get to know his dad again," she replied.

There was to be no more leave but, within a year, the war was almost over. The work at Winslow had in part brought the Nazis down. When peace was finally declared, Winslow began winding down its operations.

Dreading his return to being a baker's rounds man, Fred was thrilled when Gaffer called him into his office and offered him a position with a research facility in Essex. He could hardly believe his luck. Finally, he was going to make something of himself and he could take care of his family properly. They'd all survived, now he could look ahead at the possibilities this new job offered. He couldn't wait to tell Jo.

Fred returned home elated. It was time to pick up the pieces of family life, but it wouldn't be easy. After keeping secrets for over a year, he was still unable to speak about his work at Winslow and now his new job would be just as secret.

With rationing still severe, as it would be for quite some time, Jo was anxious to put something special on the table for Fred's return. She'd been diligent with her vegetable garden and filled her pot with the ingredients for a stew, but there was very little meat.

Edna's husband wasn't due back for several weeks and, upon hearing Jo's woes, gave up her precious piece of stewing beef to add to the pot. Adding lardy dumplings, Jo had a substantial, if unexciting, meal ready for Fred's first meal as a civilian. It was wonderful to sit down to a midday dinner together once again. Jimmy for once, behaved himself at the table, and when they'd all finished, Fred declared that was best meal ever!

Once Jimmy had disappeared from the table to play with his toy spitfire by the fire, Jo uneasily broached the subject of work. "Will you get your job back at the co-op, Fred?" she asked tentatively, knowing he dreaded it, but at the same time, no one could be choosy.

Grinning broadly, Fred shook his head. "No," he announced triumphantly. "I won't, but I have a job and you'll never guess where!"

"Come on, don't keep me in suspense! What's going on?"

"I've been offered a position with the MOD in research—and it's on Foulness Island! But that's all I can tell you, so please don't ask me for any details."

"But that's wonderful, and it's only a bus ride away. Oh, Fred, I'm so proud of you. When do you start?"

"In a couple of weeks, so let's make the most of the time off. Come on, Jimmy, let's go and see them taking down the barbed wire on the beach," Fred suggested.

"Well, that's an exciting way to celebrate the end of the war and a new job!" Jo exclaimed.

The three of them started walking toward the beach, going past the Edwardian band stage to the cliff path.

"Did you know I lived along here, opposite the park, when I was little, 'til Sid died," Jo said wistfully.

"No kidding. My gran lived along here, but I never knew her. She died when I was just a lad," Fred said.

Jo suddenly stopped and stared at a *For Sale* board tied to the garden railings of one of the houses.

"Oh, that's my house!" she cried excitedly pointing to one of the attractive buildings. "Yes, that's the right number. I wish we could live here. I have such lovely memories. Do you think we could afford to buy it, Fred?"

"Be nice, wouldn't it? Sort of coming full circle. We'll see, tomorrow," he replied. "After all, we have all the time in the world now."

About the Author

Vivienne Barker, born and raised in England, art college dropout, fish and chip fryer, civil servant, library technician and much more, is now retired to the beautiful Kawartha Lakes area of Ontario, Canada. Having worked for "the man" all her adult life, she decided to finally do what *she* wanted, which was to look after animals. Her company *Four on the Floor (and a Tail)* was a passion for five years prior to retirement.

At a party, she was asked to speak about family origins and any interesting events therein. Friends were intrigued and said she should write a book. So she did. *The Train Now Leaving*, although classed as fiction is actually semibiographical in that almost all the characters actually existed and most of the events actually happened. Her short story "The Shaman's Prophecy" is included in the *Kawartha Lakes Writers Summer Anthology*, and "Footprints in the Snow" has been accepted for the *Winter Anthology* 2017-2018. She also has a story "The Verdict is In" included in *Shorelines* published by Polar Expressions.

When not scribbling, she can be found walking her dog Cassie along the lakeshore, creating an English garden (how foolish in a northern Ontario climate!), and sitting on her deck enjoying the view (and the odd gin and tonic!)

Made in the USA
Columbia, SC
06 May 2017